W9-BNE-196

THE PRETTIEST

ALSO BY BRIGIT YOUNG

• • • • • • • • • • • •

Worth a Thousand Words

THE PRETTIEST

BRIGIT YOUNG

ROARING BROOK PRESS
New York

Published by Roaring Brook Press
Roaring Brook Press is a division of
Holtzbrinck Publishing Holdings Limited Partnership
120 Broadway, New York, NY 10271
mackids.com

Library of Congress Control Number: 2019941020

ISBN 9781626729230

Our books may be purchased in bulk for promotional, educational, or business use. Please contact your local bookseller or the Macmillan Corporate and Premium Sales Department at (800) 221-7945 ext. 5442 or by email at MacmillanSpecialMarkets@macmillan.com.

First edition, 2020
Book design by Cassie Gonzales
Printed in the United States of America

3 5 7 9 10 8 6 4 2

For my mom, Brady.
Back when I was in middle school you told me I should write about it. You were right.

I am trying to find myself. Sometimes that's not easy.

—Marilyn Monroe

THE PRETTIEST

1

EVE

Eve could feel them staring.

As the homeroom bell rang on Monday morning, the room filled with the buzz of cell phones. When Eve looked around to see what was going on, dozens of eyes pointed in her direction. It was as if a spotlight had illuminated her.

Eve focused on the notebook in front of her, ignoring the rising commotion in the room. She didn't want to know why a few girls in the back of homeroom had begun to cry and some boys had started to snicker, or why the back of her head had suddenly become so fascinating to people. Whatever was happening, it couldn't be good.

"Enough," Eve heard Mr. Flynn groan. "Phones *down*."

The room ignored him. Eve picked up a pen.

Over the summer, each student had to choose a person to read about for the biography project they'd be doing in eighth grade. At one of Eve's weekly trips to the library, she'd discovered a dusty, old collection of Emily Dickinson's poems and chosen her. And then one night, Eve scratched a pen over a blank page, and before she knew it, she had filled a notebook with poetry of her own. But she'd never shown a soul, not even her best friend, Nessa. No way.

That morning, she attempted a poetry exercise she'd read about in one of her thoroughly dog-eared creative writing manuals, in which you take a line from a famous poem and try to write your own poem following it.

The line, by Walt Whitman, read: *I am large, I contain multitudes . . .*

Eve tried to think of a line to follow.

I am large, she began writing. Well, she *felt* large recently, at least certain parts of her body did. This past summer had been what Nessa called Eve's "summer of the curves." Her clothing size had significantly altered, and she wore a lot of her big brother's old shirts these days.

"I contain multitudes . . ." What did that even mean?

I contain, she tried again.

But as she wrote, Mr. Flynn hovered by her desk, his fingertips grazing the edge of her notebook.

She looked up, expecting a rebuke, the usual reminder that she needed to pay attention. But Mr. Flynn merely stood there, surveying the scene. "What's going on here?" he asked the room.

Eve forced herself to look around and had the same question.

One girl openly wept.

Two boys huddled around a phone, cackling and crying out "Oh man!"

And several kids sat there peering directly at Eve.

It seemed like they'd noticed her for the first time. One girl, Mari, glared at her as if Eve were a new dark mole appearing after a day in the sun, and a boy named Auggie gawked at her like she'd manifested out of thin air in a puff of smoke.

She snapped back to her paper.

Why were they looking at her?

Words. Focus on words.

I am large, I contain multitudes.

Once more, Eve tried to write what came next.

But they were still staring. She could feel it. The eyes shooting stares at the back of her head felt like hot sparks of oil spritzing off a stove onto her skin.

"Okay, can someone please fill me in?" Mr. Flynn mumbled as one of the kids offered him her phone.

His eyes widened. "Oh lord," Mr. Flynn murmured, glued to the screen.

Eve registered a tap on her shoulder. The tap belonged to Miranda Garland, the girl who had sat behind her for over two years of homeroom. They'd hardly spoken before.

"Hey," Miranda said. "I've been meaning to ask you for a long time . . . Where did you get that necklace with the little hand? It's so cute."

Eve did one of those "Are you talking to me?" gestures, and Miranda nodded.

"From my grandmother?" Eve answered, hesitant. Her bubbe had given it to her for her bat mitzvah over the summer, and the little hamsa hung on a silver chain around her neck every day. It was no big deal. Why was Miranda suddenly interested in this?

Out of the corner of her eye, Eve caught a face in the classroom door's window. It was Nessa, motioning for her to come out.

Eve glanced toward Nessa and then Mr. Flynn. He stood next to a group of distraught kids, distracted. Eve sneaked out the classroom door.

"Did you see the list?" Nessa pulled Eve in close.

Maybe it was all about the cast list. Mr. Rhodes was supposed to announce the cast for *The Music Man* any day now. Maybe there'd been an upset, an unexpected casting decision. Eve momentarily worried for Nessa, the lead contender for the role of Marian the librarian. Nessa was "born to be a Broadway diva," she'd always say, whereas standing on a stage in front of a bunch of people probably qualified as Eve's worst nightmare.

"You got the part, right?" Eve asked.

"No! Well, I mean, I'm sure I did. But that's not the list I'm talking about."

Nessa handed Eve her phone.

And in the glow of Nessa's screen, Eve saw it. She took in the series of numbers in tiny type, one to fifty, and there, in the number one spot, she saw her own name.

"It's a list of the top fifty girls in eighth grade," Nessa whispered.

"But my last name starts with *H*!" Eve felt stupid even as she spoke, already knowing that she was far behind on whatever was going on.

"It's the top fifty *prettiest*, Evie." Nessa put a hand on her shoulder, pointing to the heading of the list where THE PRETTIEST 8TH GRADERS OF FORD MIDDLE SCHOOL had been typed out in all caps. "You're number one."

Impossible.

It was true that Eve didn't *hate* the way she looked. She liked her tight, coffee-colored curls and the way they lay on her shoulders. But her new body presented a person light years away from the person Eve felt like inside. She wanted to slide by, unnoticed, pretty enough but not too pretty, for as long as she could.

So "number one prettiest"? No way. Eve could think of a hundred other girls who deserved that spot.

All those thoughts swirled in her brain in a millisecond and came out of her mouth in a "Huh?" right as Brody Dixon, the school-wide idol of sixth and seventh grade groupies, strutted by and stopped where Eve and Nessa stood.

He flicked a hall pass against his palm.

Slap. Slap. Slap.

"Hey, *Eve Hoffman*." He said her name as if he was trying the sounds out for the first time to see how they felt coming from his mouth. "Congrats." He continued on his saunter down the hallway.

At this, Eve slid back inside the classroom door just in

time to hear Mr. Flynn end some kind of speech to three of the boys in the back of the classroom.

"This is an unacceptable way for anyone to behave!" he boomed. "Out in the real world, this would get you fired from a job. Here, maybe it'll get you expelled. You know what? The bell's going to ring any minute. Just pack up your things."

He turned to Eve and gave her a look she interpreted as "I'm so sorry for what's about to happen to you."

And what would happen?

As Eve jammed her notebook into her backpack, she did everything she could to avoid meeting all those leering faces.

She repeated Walt Whitman's line over and over to herself, like a prayer. "I am large, I am large, I am large . . ." But they were the wrong words for that day. Because if she could have made one wish in that moment, it would have been to drink the potion that Alice takes in Wonderland and turn so small that she disappeared entirely.

2

SOPHIE

Every day, Sophie woke up an hour and a half before she had to get on the bus. She had perfected the art of the blowout. It took her only fifteen minutes to section, curl, brush, and spray her hair into a swishy blond mane that would make a pop star jealous. Then came her makeup, which consumed the largest chunk of her time. She applied three shades of bronze eye shadow, and then chocolate brown eyeliner, drawing it not only above and below her lashes, but also in the hidden creases right under the lids. That really made her blue eyes pop. And last, she lined and lipsticked her mouth with her signature magenta pink. Her makeup skills were a true gift. By the time she left for school, she looked so put together that once in a while, on her way to the bus stop, even a high school guy or two would stare.

Once she was at Ford, she owned the place. She got all As. That was a given. She was the best one on the track team, training all year to maximize her speed. One day she planned to get a track scholarship to the University of Michigan. And all the boys loved her. It was just a fact. Brody Dixon, who looked like a tenth grader and lived in the biggest house in all of Glisgold, had a thing for her. He'd been openly flirting all year, even having her over to study, and everyone knew they'd go to the Halloween dance together. In all the ways that counted, she was number one. In everything.

When the list came out that morning, Sophie Kane stood leaning against her locker, surrounded by her girls, many of them ready to take a tardy in homeroom just to wait by her side until the last minute. And they were *her* girls. They may have had their own names—Amina, Liv, Hayley, plus a few others who mattered less—but everyone called them "the Sophies." They would never call *themselves* this, out in the open, but people referred to them this way behind their backs. And Sophie knew that if other people said it, then it became the truth. So they were hers.

As the Sophies babbled about something or other, Sophie

played with a Spanish app on her phone. She had to work on her Spanish. The new verbs confused her. They were impossible to memorize, especially with how little she'd been sleeping lately. And falling behind was not an option, not for her.

As she moved to the future irregular tense, a few "Oh my Gods" whooshed around her, and texts of screenshots of the list poured onto her phone in a flood, drowning out tener and tendré, and as the reality of the image hit her, as the rankings sank in and she saw that she was not number one, but number two—*number two!*—Sophie smiled a perfectly practiced smile and let the world believe that she was totally, entirely, and completely fine.

But Sophie Kane was not fine.

Sophie had been wronged.

"Guys, this is so dumb," she chirped to the girls as they nodded in agreement. "And Rose Reed is number four?" she asked. "*Rose*?" Rose, already in her homeroom, was one of the Sophies who mattered less. She wore pink belts every day.

"She's not even that pretty!" insisted Amina, a generally easygoing girl who Sophie liked. Amina had been ranked as number three. Probably about right. She had incredible skin and lashes to die for.

But Rose? She was only around them at all because one of

Brody Dixon's best friends, Caleb Rhines, was into her. Rose sat on the edges of their lunch table, staring at Sophie with a lingering gaze that freaked her out. At least *pretend* you're not obsessed with me, Sophie always thought.

"And Eve Hoffman is a weirdo," said Hayley, number five, one of the most airheaded girls on the planet. Hayley was gorgeous and the best athlete in the grade, but every time she spoke Sophie had to stop herself from just getting up and walking away. "She never pays attention, and when she's called on in class she just gives this dumb look like . . ." And Hayley did an impression of someone without a thought in her head. So basically, Sophie thought, just an impression of herself.

"That's true," Liv agreed. Liv, number six, was the smartest of the Sophies. Her long box braids perfectly framed a heart-shaped face.

"Whatever, I'm heading in to homeroom." Sophie flipped her hair to land behind her back. "Ignore this," she commanded to the teary-eyed girls. Crying bothered Sophie. A lot.

But Sophie didn't head to homeroom. As she neared the door to it, she dashed into the bathroom instead, running into the final stall. Some girls were hiding in there. She could hear nose blowing. Sophie wasn't a hider like them. She just needed a moment alone. She lifted her feet onto the porcelain.

Eve Hoffman? Number one? The quiet girl, her face always in a book, who lurked around the theater kids? Sophie Kane, number two?

It didn't make any sense!

Sophie's mom always said, "Don't ever let anyone think you're *less than*."

And she never did.

So how could she be number two? How had this happened?

What would people think? What would Brody Dixon think?

Whoever was in the stall next to her sounded like she was at the beginning of a panic attack. She could hear the hurried breath, and it reminded her of a mouse, and how their hearts beat hundreds of times a minute.

People were so weak.

Sophie, sitting with her knees pulled up to her chest, stuffed her tears deep down inside. She placed them in the same spot she parked the image of her increasingly empty mailbox, which each month received fewer and fewer postcards from her dad, and the exhaustion she felt in the mornings, when it took everything in her to pull out a hair dryer and start the day.

No. Tears.

She whipped out her mirror. It had a crack in the upper corner that distorted the image of her perfectly plucked right eyebrow. She pulled out her magenta lipstick. It was down to its last little bit, and she silently cursed. She could feel the cold metal edges of the tube's rim as she painted it onto her mouth. When she got home, she'd scrape out the last bits and put them in a little baggie, a trick her mom taught her. Then it would last a few more days.

Sophie smacked her lips together, put her wedges onto the floor, took a breath, and walked out.

She would find out who wrote this list. And she'd destroy them. She'd make them a joke. She'd get a new list written. She'd ensure she was number one. She'd never, ever let anyone see her as "less than."

3

EVE

"They say," Nessa gossiped to Eve over lunch as they huddled together at a corner table, "that Lara Alexander went home in tears."

"She's not on the list?" Eve asked. Seeing Nessa's look, Eve explained, "I haven't looked at the whole thing. I couldn't. But that's weird!"

Even Eve knew that Lara Alexander was remarkably well dressed, and Eve hardly noticed that stuff. Plus, her dad was the first African American president of the hospital. There had been all these announcements about it in the paper a couple of years back. Her mom wrote cookbooks. Famous ones. Her sister was the most popular girl in the high school. Lara seemed like someone who should be included in everything.

"Well, she left school after second period. Guess *somebody* expected a spot, huh?" Nessa raised an eyebrow. Then her face fell. "This is all pretty messed up."

Eve nodded. Looking around them she saw that they weren't the only pair of friends nestled more tightly together that day, as if by physically sticking closely to one another they could create a shield from staring eyes, from the rankings. And the lack-of-rankings. But even as everyone stuck to their friendship groups, they also checked out one another, gauging the reactions of the other girls in school, and watching how the boys responded. Some kids leaned their heads in toward one another, speaking in hushed whispers, just like Eve and Nessa were doing. Brody Dixon held court as usual, telling a story with wild hand motions, taking up all the oxygen in the lunchroom. His crowd of worshippers guffawed at whatever he was saying.

"Oh, good. Looks like *he's* having a *great* day," Nessa muttered, looking off toward the same spot as Eve.

Farther down the table, though, where Sophie Kane sat with the Sophies, things looked more solemn. They ate in near silence.

Rose Reed put a hand on Sophie Kane's shoulder, and Eve might have been imagining it, but she thought she saw Sophie stiffen.

"Sophie Kane must hate you," Nessa whispered.

"Oh my gosh, you're right," Eve said. "I hadn't even thought of that."

The two of them sat with this for a moment, and quickly turned away when a couple of the Sophies glanced toward their corner.

"What do you think Principal Yu is going to say at the assembly?" Nessa wondered aloud before blowing bubbles into her grape juice.

An assembly had been called for the eighth graders in place of last period to "discuss, as a community, the incident earlier today," Principal Yu told them over the loudspeakers.

"Who knows? But whatever it is, it won't make a difference." Eve glanced back one last time at the Sophies. Sophie stared at her, her made-up face unreadable. Eve jumped a little in her seat.

She turned to Nessa. "What do I do about Sophie Kane?"

Nessa shrugged. "Like my dad always says: 'This, too, shall pass.'"

"Oh, great."

Miranda Garland and one of her friends walked by their

table and waved at Eve, ignoring Nessa. Eve lifted a hand in response, trying not to grimace at the awkwardness of it all.

"Well, ex*cuse* me," Nessa said under her breath.

"Was Miranda on the list?" Eve asked.

Nessa eyed her phone. "Nope." She shook her head. "Who wrote this stupid thing, I wonder? The account name is LordTesla. Creepy!"

But Eve had retreated into her own little world. "There's this famous Emily Dickinson poem . . . ," she began, and Nessa sighed.

"Here we go with Emily again." Nessa returned to blowing bubbles.

"What? I love her, okay?" As Eve pushed around her fruit salad with a fork, she recited: "It goes, *I'm nobody! Who are you? Are you nobody, too?*"

"Please get to the part where I'm supposed to understand."

"Okay, okay, fine. Then, in the end of the poem, it says, *How dreary to be somebody. How public, like a frog. To tell one's name, the livelong June, to an admiring bog* . . . Get it?"

Nessa giggled. "Huh? A *bog*? Nope. Don't get it at all. Aw. I love my weird little bookworm." She leaned in to Eve, and they folded into each other for a moment with the perfect ease and comfort of best friends since kindergarten.

But Eve broke out of their embrace.

"Don't you understand? I was 'Nobody,' but I'm . . . 'Somebody' now! And that's . . . well, a problem!"

Nessa just stared at her.

"My name will be called out all day to the bog? Like, the school is the bog? Get it . . . ?"

Nessa began to say something, but rising voices from the popular table stopped her.

"Aw, come on, cheer up, you got silver!" Brody Dixon yelled over a half-dozen heads toward Sophie Kane.

"What did you say?" Sophie responded, her eyes furious slits.

"Man, what an Ice Queen . . . ," Nessa murmured to Eve.

"Silver medal!" Brody continued. "A place on the podium! So why the long face?"

"The face is the problem," Caleb Rhines quipped from Brody's side.

The boys cackled. Except for one, Eve noticed. He just sat there, eating his food. He looked up, and their eyes met, and she felt her face flush. He'd caught her in a full-on stare. Whoops.

"Who's the one with the glasses again?" Eve turned to Nessa.

"Winston Byrd, I think? Wins all the science awards." Nessa shook her head, still watching the popular table. "It's so stupid. Because Sophie is so obviously pretty. Who cares, anyway?"

"Which part do you think is stupid? Sophie being upset about the list or Brody being a Malfoy about it?"

"Malfoy" was the word they'd been using for "jerk" ever since they'd read *Harry Potter* together in second grade.

"Both, obviously."

Within a flash, as if nothing had been said, Brody picked up his tray and slid in by Sophie. He rustled her blond hair, and she smacked his arm in mock anger. Brody's constant followers, Caleb, Tariq, and Aidan, each slid in between pairs of Sophies. Winston stayed where he was.

Popular kids were so confusing.

Hollers, sobs, and jeers bounced off the walls of the auditorium.

When Principal Yu finally quieted the entire eighth grade down, sniffles could still be heard.

"I've called you all here today to discuss an act of extreme disrespect. I will admit that I am truly saddened by this incident," Principal Yu began, the school's disappointed parent.

Eve and Nessa sat in the second-to-last row with all three-hundred-and-something kids. Eve rested her forehead on her hand to draw zero attention to herself. But despite this effort, Curtis Milford bent into the space between Eve's and Nessa's ears and whispered, "Who put you as number one, anyway? You wrote the list yourself, huh?"

Eve winced at the closeness of his voice.

Nessa shooed Curtis away with her hand.

He leaned back, and another boy sitting next to him said, "She's number one because she's frickin' perfect, dude. Look at her!"

"Will you guys go back to the toxic-waste bin you crawled out of?" Nessa snapped too loudly, causing a third of the auditorium to glance at them.

Even Principal Yu stopped speaking for half a second and looked their way before continuing.

Eve slumped lower in her chair.

"Sorry." Nessa shrugged. "I don't like people getting that close to my ears." Then she mouthed, "Personal space" as she motioned around herself.

Curtis Milford had always seemed nice. Nice *enough*. Not that they ever spoke much, but they'd known each other since they were about eight. They'd played clarinet together in fifth grade band. He'd been on her sixth grade group report on Morocco. Why would he think that she wrote the list?

Eve tuned back in to Principal Yu's speech.

"What went on today," Principal Yu said with a sigh, "will not be tolerated."

The kids generally loved Principal Yu. She was even nice to bullies who went to the Planning Zone, which really meant detention, giving them high fives and stuff as they went about their days. They may have technically had a school counselor, but Principal Yu played that role, too. That day, though, Principal Yu's fingers clutched her papers so hard that Eve imagined her fingertips might turn white. She didn't seem like someone you'd want to talk to about *anything*.

"All your parents have already been contacted, and they have all been invited to a community school meeting to be held here tomorrow evening. I highly encourage you to join them." A few kids groaned at the mention of parents. But Principal Yu continued over their protestations. "For now, in terms of how we will deal with this as a community of learners at this institution, there will be antibullying sessions in every homeroom later in the week, as well as a presentation in each homeroom tomorrow on the effects of sexual harassment."

At the word "sexual," several kids laughed.

Eve couldn't stop herself from looking around to see

where Sophie Kane sat. She spotted several blond heads, but not Sophie's.

"For the next couple of weeks, students will immediately be granted a hall pass to go see the school counselor at any time if they wish to do so. Additionally"—and Principal Yu raised her voice as the focus of the eighth graders waned—"and you better listen to this part, everybody: This will be the *last chance* for the writer or writers of this list to set things straight. You know the drill, folks. Come forward now, on your own, and the punishment will be relatively light. Wait for us to find you—and we *will* find you—and serious consequences are on the table. Harassment will not stand here at Ford. Please," Principal Yu pleaded with them, "be kinder to one another."

As the assembly ended and kids shot out of their seats to head home, Eve kept her head down and scurried past Curtis Milford and his friend. Curtis thought she wrote the list herself, that she was an attention seeker. His little buddy thought she was "frickin' perfect." Both felt gross.

Nessa's mom drove them home. Eve and Nessa lived a block away from each other, and their parents took turns picking them up from school when it was cold. In the spring, they walked home by themselves, stopping at the grocery store along the way and noshing on the free samples. All winter long, Eve and Nessa dreamed of freedom and cubed cheese.

Nessa's mom asked how they were doing, and they assured her they were fine, but Eve could tell that Mrs. Flores-Brady was worried. Normally, Nessa's mom was good at pretending to be interested when Nessa went on and on about theater and movies, but that day, as Nessa chattered away about the new cast of *Hamilton*, Eve thought she noticed a strain in Mrs. Flores-Brady's "Oh yeahs?"

As the car rolled into Eve's driveway, Nessa's mom motioned for Eve to lean up to the front to kiss her cheek.

"Vaya mi vida, que dios te acompañe," she cooed to Eve as their cheeks touched.

Nessa's mom often said goodbye with "may God be with you" to Eve, and Eve grinned as she heard Nessa reply: "Mama, God hung out with me and Eve earlier. He's got other stuff to do tonight. Big world out there."

As Eve hopped out of the car, she imagined Nessa's chuckle and her mom's eye roll, and she smiled to herself.

There was no laughter in Eve's house that night as her family discussed the list over dinner.

"I don't understand," her mom said. "Why would someone do this?"

"Because middle school boys are imbeciles, Mom," Eve's older brother, Abe, insisted. "I mean— "

Speaking over him, her dad teased, "And you're a grown man now, huh?"

"I'm serious," Abe persisted. "The sooner girls figure out that the boys around them just don't value their inner truth, then maybe they'll find a little confidence. A little self-love, you know? Eve—just ignore this crap."

"Abe! Watch it!" Her dad didn't care so much about curse words, but he knew it bugged her mom. And in her house, even "crap" was unacceptable.

"And why should she ignore it?" her dad went on, a smirk back on his face, as if Abe amused him. "She's number one! Your sister is the prettiest girl in school. I've always known that. And, hey, don't forget, while you're giving your sermon over there, that your job is to protect her. Right?" He smacked Abe on the back.

Abe shook his head, his mop of brown hair falling in front of his eyes. "Dad, you're a part of the problem."

The smile disappeared from her dad's face. "And what's that supposed to mean?"

Before her dad could continue, Eve's little sister, Hannah, jumped in.

"I think it's awesome. Evie, how did you do it? I mean,

seriously, you are the exact opposite of cool, and now this all of a sudden?! What happened? Is it the . . ." And Hannah motioned in front of her chest.

"Hannah!" scolded her mom.

Eve's mom liked to say that Hannah was ten going on sixteen. However old she was or wasn't, she was definitely annoying. She spent about twenty minutes doing her hair in the morning, hogging the bathroom.

"What happened is someone decided to objectify our sister," Abe lectured Hannah like a concerned teacher. "And Dad doesn't seem to care," he added under his breath.

"And what does 'objectify' even mean?" Hannah asked, but not in the way that sounded like she actually wanted the answer. Hannah had the ability to ask questions in a voice that said, "You should really shut up."

"It means," Abe answered anyway, growing heated, "that someone decided to treat her like an *object*. They ranked her like you'd rank video games, like 'Top Fifty RPF Games,' or like how you'd rate an action figure on Amazon, ignoring that she's a *human being*." He pounded the table and dropped his fork. "Jesus, it's so sick."

"Abe!" Eve's mom snapped. "Enough with the language!"

"Really? That one? Whatever," he muttered, and returned to shoveling food in his mouth, quickly and ferociously, as if he were about to run a marathon. Ever since he'd hit high school, he could consume three portions and still be hungry a couple of hours later, searching the fridge at all hours of the night. It drove Eve crazy when there were leftovers of her favorite dish for her lunch the next day, but Abe went on a midnight raid, and by morning they were all gone.

"Well, I think it's a compliment," Hannah chirped.

"It is!" Her dad put a hand on Hannah's. "And I don't need a list to tell me that my daughters are the most beautiful girls in the world."

He smiled warmly at Eve, but her stomach churned. She didn't quite know why.

Abe rolled his eyes and prepared for a debate, but their mom's glare quieted him. Her mom hated fighting, which was too bad because her family bickered pretty much every night.

"Is Nessa super sad that you're number one and she's not even on it?" Hannah asked, chewing as she spoke.

"No!" Eve scoffed. "We're best friends!"

And it hit Eve that she didn't actually know the answer. Nessa hadn't *seemed* sad that day, but she should have asked Nessa how the list had made her feel. Eve had been so wrapped up in herself that she was acting exactly like the kind of girl who *would* be number one on a "prettiest" list, like a Sophie, only thinking about who was staring at her and when and why.

Later that night, flopping on her bed, she texted Nessa. **Hey. I'm such a total Malfoy for not asking how you're feeling about this stupid list.**

Before Nessa could even respond, Eve added, **You know you're so pretty, right?**

lolololol, Nessa wrote back. **thanks ill keep that in my heart 4ever**

Eve giggled and sent a GIF of some goofy-looking guy shrugging.

Nessa responded with a GIF of a model strutting down the runway and flipping her hair.

im fine, obvs, Nessa wrote. **look its not a secret that a bigger girl isnt going to be in the top 50. or 100. haha not at ford at least**

Eve sent a mad face. **IT'S SO STUPID**! she added. And she knew better than to say Nessa wasn't big. Nothing annoyed Nessa more. If Eve protested, "You're not 'bigger'!" it implied there was something *wrong* with being big. And there wasn't. At all.

You are beautiful! Eve texted. Ugh. Was that the right thing to say, or did she sound like she was trying too hard?

Maybe there was *no* right thing to say. She opened the picture of the list on her phone and stared at the absence of Nessa's name.

It had been a horrible day, but that absence was the worst part.

As if reading her thoughts, Nessa responded, **if you feel bad for me, you're making it worse. i mean it, okay? i. don't. care. i can guarantee you i am the one person in that school who will win an oscar (no offense) and you're all going to wish you were me, so it doesn't really matter what sophie kanes little boyfriends think right now**

I'm hugging you. Eve smiled and pressed the phone to her cheek.

me too number one. omg my mom is downstairs praying for us right now hahaha

I'm sure mine is, too! Eve wrote. **Sigh.**

That night, as Eve's mom surely lay in bed whispering the *Sh'ma*, Nessa's mom would be praying in front of her altar, laying down some freshly bought flowers before the cross.

They had always shared this, their God-fearing moms. Their God-neutral dads.

And, like Nessa's mom, Eve's mother was always full of

concerns: about Abe, that he wasn't humble enough, about Hannah, that she cared so much about her looks. And, until today, she'd worried that Eve kept her head in her books and out of the world. But now, she'd probably worry about Eve's newfound status as "the prettiest."

Eve wished she could just go back to being *nobody*, back to her usual spot as the quiet middle child, as the silent sidekick behind Nessa, and not shift to *somebody*, her name croaked out by the frogs into the bog of Ford Middle School.

4

SOPHIE

The next morning Sophie woke to the sound of her sister's snores.

She slipped out of their shared room, down the hall to where her mom lay fast asleep after a long night of work.

Sophie crawled under her mom's covers. Her mom's arm draped over her.

"Hey," her mom whispered into Sophie's hair.

"Hey."

Sophie's mom still smelled like french fry grease and coffee grounds.

"You okay, sweet girl?"

"Yeah."

"Got some email from Ford," her mom mumbled, turning onto her back, her eyes still closed.

Sophie propped herself up and looked at her mom. Her mom was so beautiful, even all smelly from the diner and with her dark brown roots starting to show. Her lips reminded Sophie of the way little kids drew mouths on faces, in a heart shape. She looked like she should be in one of those old movies with a scarf wrapped around her head, big sunglasses on, wearing a white, billowy dress. One time, when her mom was in high school, a modeling talent scout had given her his business card. Even though nothing came of it, Sophie loved that story.

She took in the faded brown smudges on her mom's lids where hours ago there'd been carefully applied bronze eye shadow.

She should let her rest.

"Yeah. The whole thing is ridiculous, Mom," Sophie whispered, kissing her forehead. "Don't worry."

As Sophie got up to leave, her mom said, "Go get 'em, honey," and she put a pillow over her head as she went back to sleep.

Sophie headed to the bathroom to begin her morning routine. Today she had to look better than ever. She had to make the whole school look at her and Eve Nobody Hoffman and think, "This list is meaningless." She had to look like number one, and even more importantly, act like it. No weakness.

She turned on her morning playlist and lip-synched at her reflection until she saw her face become stunning and felt her spine turn to steel.

When she finished, dressed up in her best outfit—a scarlet shirt she'd found for only three bucks at Goodwill and some cute new pants she'd saved up for with her babysitting money—she went to wake up Bella.

"Come on, Bel! Time to get up! And put on that skirt I made you! It's finished!"

Sophie cooked them scrambled eggs, and they headed off to school.

She pictured Ford as it would be at that moment, at seven o'clock A.M., unlit, with no students in it. Empty. It made her think of the old battlefields they read about in history class: a long grassy valley, all quiet, birds singing just like normal. And then a loud roar would come as two sides came toward one another ready to fight.

Sophie and her sister were the first kids on the bus. Sophie was the only kid at Ford who lived in Silver Ledge

Apartments. The rest of the Silver Ledge kids were in elementary or high school.

"Don't let anyone know where you live," their mom always told them. "People in schools like yours will judge you for it. Trust me."

And only a couple of kids did know, the ones who boarded at the stop after them. Luckily, they'd kept quiet so far.

Silver Ledge sat at the border of town, teetering between school districts. The rent was high, way higher than if they moved a few streets away to the apartments in Oakwood, but Sophie knew her mom stayed there because she wanted Sophie and Bella to go to the better public schools, even if it meant extra night shifts. Her dad sent money sometimes, and that helped, too, when it came.

As the bus rode farther into town, the houses grew bigger and bigger, until eventually they passed by Brody Dixon's place, which was practically a castle. He not only had a bedroom for each sibling, and an office for his dad's fancy job, and a room with a huge TV with every video game you could think of, he also had a room that—no joke—only the dog slept in. A dog room.

She'd noticed it last week, on a day he'd invited her over to do homework, back when she'd been the prettiest. A day when he'd leaned toward her, his mouth all puckered and hopeful. And pushy.

As they passed by his mansion, Bella elbowed Sophie and made smooching noises.

"Oh, shut up." But Sophie smiled.

Bella did this nearly every day.

Would she stop doing it if Brody started ignoring Sophie? Would he ever ask her over again? Would he be too embarrassed to go to the Halloween dance with number two?

Sophie pulled out her cracked pocket mirror and checked her face. She swiveled her profile side to side. The full inspection. Perfectly even foundation, blended down to midneck. Perfect, bright eyes. Lips painted a perfect pink. Perfect.

She ruffled Bella's hair as her sister hopped off at the elementary school.

And as the bus pulled up to Ford, she gave her reflection one last glance in the window and headed into battle.

5

EVE

The crowds parted for Sophie Kane, like a queen among peasants. Eve could see the back of her yellow hair, bouncing behind her. Was it possible for hair to sparkle? Sophie's did.

And then, as Eve and Nessa waved bye to Eve's mom and climbed out of the car, something strange began to happen. The crowd parted for them, too. Small groups split off and tightened, whispering to one another as Eve and Nessa walked by the bust of Henry Ford and through the school's enormous front doors.

Eve slouched her shoulders forward, attempting to sink in her chest and disappear into Abe's Detroit Pistons T-shirt.

"What do you think they're saying?" she murmured to Nessa. "Do you think they think I wrote the list? It really bugs me that Curtis thinks I wrote the list."

"Who cares?" Nessa answered. "This, too, shall pass," she mouthed to Eve as they parted ways for homeroom.

Easier said than done. Why didn't Nessa get that?

As Eve headed down the hallway, she felt her phone buzz and saw a text from an unknown number. It read: **u look real good today**

Eve checked all around her. Who had her number? Who was watching her?

Inside Mr. Flynn's class, the bright overhead bulb made it feel like an interrogation room. No one was crying this morning. Instead, they stared at Eve. Miranda Garland smiled and waved. Eve saw that Miranda wore a necklace with a gold hamsa on it. How'd she get one so fast? *Why'd* she get one?

A woman in a tight pencil skirt and a white blouse stood at the front of Mr. Flynn's desk. Behind her, Eve saw a PowerPoint presentation had been set up.

WHAT IS SEXUAL HARASSMENT? it read.

The boy next to her jiggled his knee and bit his fingernails.

The woman introduced herself and launched into her routine. "I've been brought here today, along with my colleagues currently in the other classrooms, to talk to you all about an incident that occurred yesterday. Who here knows what sexual harassment is?"

She said "harassment" with an emphasis on the first syllable—*hair*issment—and a few snickers could be heard around the room.

As she continued, every time she said "*hair*issment," which was a lot, the giggles grew louder and louder.

Eve took out her notebook, pretended to take notes, and instead secretly scribbled poems.

When the bell rang, Mr. Flynn called her over. He waited to speak until everyone was gone.

"How are you doing?" he asked.

Eve felt herself blush. She always blushed, even if she wasn't embarrassed. It was like her face was trying to tell the rest of her body to hide.

"I'm fine," she answered.

The thought of Mr. Flynn looking at her face and thinking about how someone had called her the prettiest girl in the school filled her with dread. Was he thinking, "How could this awkward kid be prettiest?" Was it weird of Eve to even wonder that? Was he judging her just like everyone else was? Did he think she wrote the list herself?

"I just wanted to remind you that the counselors are available to talk. That's their job, you know." His eyebrows furrowed in that kind of ultraconcern that you never want to see on a grown-up's face.

"Yup," Eve mumbled.

"Okay . . . And Principal Yu is available, too," he added. He seemed to want this conversation even less than Eve did.

"Thanks. I'm fine, though." Eve held her notebook and schoolwork tight to her body and rushed out the door into the gawking crowds.

Out of the corner of her eye, Eve saw that sparkly blond hair again, reflecting glints of hallway light. And Eve gasped aloud as she saw that underneath the tips of Sophie's hair, a piece of paper had been taped onto her dark red shirt, the loud black Sharpie on it yelling out **#2**.

6

SOPHIE

Sophie felt a hand on her back and turned around to see the short, mousy Eve Hoffman standing before her.

It was bad enough that Eve Hoffman even felt she could talk to her in the first place, but for her to *touch* Sophie? That was over the line. Who did she think she was?

Sophie had learned a long time ago, on the rare times her dad came to stay with them and was super upset with her or Bella for something, that silence could be more powerful than yelling. So she just glared.

Two enormous brown eyes looked back up at her.

"This was—was on your—your . . ." Eve Hoffman made a motion toward Sophie's back.

Eve Hoffman held a Post-it reading **#2**.

Sophie snatched the paper out of her hands and crumpled it up.

"I'm so sorry. Someone must've . . ." Eve Hoffman didn't seem to have the ability to finish a sentence.

Eve's hair was a disaster. Bits of it peeked out from every corner of her skull, covered in a light layer of frizz. She wore some kind of navy blue sports shirt and black jeans, the colors clashing. Even while dressed in a glorified bag, Sophie could see that she had what Brody called "a body." He always talked about celebrities and said some had "a body," or sometimes he'd say, "Ugh. She doesn't even have a body." Sometimes when he said this, Sophie thought, "Brody, we all have bodies. It's called . . . existing." But she kept this to herself.

Eve Hoffman clearly wanted to add something, but once again it came out in disjointed stammers.

Actually, on second thought, maybe Eve Hoffman wasn't so mousy. Her eyes were Disney-princess big. Her face had that Snow White quality about it, all fresh and super pale, but in the creamy way, not the vampire way. Her mouth and cheeks had a natural reddish blush to them. Was she not even wearing any makeup? She just . . . glowed?

And in an instant, in a sudden shift that so often happened to her, Sophie hated herself with intensity. She hated her own limp, straight hair that needed a curling iron, her tired complexion that *needed* a makeup base to look good, hated how her upper lip was so skinny that it disappeared when she smiled. She hated her muscular body, how her shoulders, arms, and legs looked like a boy's from behind. She had a body, sure, but not "a body." She was too tough-looking. And much too flat.

She was no Eve. No number one. The list was right.

Sophie clenched her fist around the Post-it. Her nails dug into her palm. She opened her mouth to speak, but before she could say anything to dismiss Eve Hoffman, Brody walked by.

Sophie allowed her frown to transform into a broad smile, though she tried to push her top lip out as she did so, to make sure it wouldn't fade into her teeth.

"Hey!" She lifted her hand to give him their typical high-five greeting. He usually smacked her hand, then put an arm around her shoulder and strode down the hall with her that way until a hall monitor yelled "No touching!"

Brody smacked her hand, but he didn't put an arm around her. Instead, he turned to Eve Hoffman.

"There you are, Eve. Eve Hoffman." He grinned.

Eve's mouth remained open, words still not coming out. She looked exactly as spacey as Hayley had reported.

Brody put his hand on Eve's arm and guided her toward the side of the hall, leaving Sophie behind. Sophie scrambled to hear what they were saying. She put an earphone in one ear to muffle the hallway chaos and leaned her other ear in their direction.

Sophie caught Brody saying: "Would you think about . . . ?"

Then she heard nothing except a gaggle of theater kids running by her, singing some obnoxious song.

In the quiet that came after, she made out: "It'll be fun."

And it dawned on her what she was witnessing.

"Okay, I'll wait. Just let me know." Brody winked as he walked away from Eve. He gave Sophie a light pat on the back and said, "See ya, Soph."

As Sophie fully took in that Brody had just asked Eve Hoffman to the Halloween dance, she knew with an immediate certainty that Eve wanted to take her place. She'd probably written the list herself. She'd been trying to put that Post-it on Sophie's back. It had all been a plot to get Brody's attention.

And as Eve slunk away and out of her sight, Sophie stared at her hard enough to let her know that she would never, ever get away with it.

7

EVE

Text message, walking into lunch, a new unknown number:

u r so perfect. Go to haloween dance w me or no? its curtis

Text message, five minutes later, same number:

sorry about yesterday u mad?

8

SOPHIE

Sophie couldn't wait for school to end, for blessed track practice, where she could run and run and just keep running, faster than everyone else, and win the race. It was also her only time away from the Sophies. She'd convinced them long ago that they shouldn't join the team. At first Hayley had resisted, but Sophie informed Hayley it might conflict with swimming practice and the swim team was sure to get into regional competitions that year. Sophie had breathed a sigh of relief when Hayley bought that argument. Track was *Sophie's* thing.

At lunch, her whole table sat quietly. At one point, out

of nowhere, Rose Reed, who had somehow popped up only a few seats away from Sophie, turned to Sophie and said: "Hey, don't worry. First is the worst, second is the best, right? We've been told that, like, forever!"

"Did I say I'm worried? What are you, ten? It's been a whole day, and we're all moving on, okay?" Sophie snapped before returning to her mashed potatoes. They gave huge portions at school. It was awesome. You didn't even have to worry about making a big dinner if you ate your whole lunch.

God, *who* would put Rose in the top ten? She wore capris in the winter with high socks. It was like a joke! Maybe that was exactly it. Maybe if Eve wasn't behind the list, then someone wrote it as an actual joke.

But the problem was that the rest of the school had to see it that way.

She tried not to look at Eve, practically glued to her theater friend at their corner table, but she couldn't help it. And she felt a strange satisfaction at seeing Miranda Garland stand by Eve, pestering her with questions. Miranda had always done everything Sophie did—copying her clothes and hairstyles nearly day by day. It was almost amazing to see her do it to someone else.

And then it wasn't. Because what would that mean for the next day? And the year ahead? If *no one* copied Sophie, then there were no more Sophies. And then there was no more Sophie Kane.

The boys joined them midlunch, as always, but, once again, Brody didn't put his arm around her. And Sophie wasn't stupid. Sophie saw clearly that within only a day, everything had changed.

9

EVE

Text message, after fifth period, unknown number:

i know you stuff your bra

10

NESSA

Nessa knew that life was about waiting for the right moment—*your* moment. Not every moment could be yours, but then when it came, it was so sweet.

Nessa got it. She got the lead, the role of Marian the librarian, like she knew she would.

The cast list hung on the choir room door.

"Two lists in two days," she heard Erin O'Brien grumble behind her. "Just great. I'll probably be Woman Number Three in the chorus."

But when Erin arrived at the list, she saw that she'd been

cast in a big role and she spun around in circles in her purple wheelchair, getting high fives from everybody.

"Congrats!" Nessa beamed as Erin smacked her palm. Well deserved. Erin had an alto voice to die for.

Yes, Nessa assumed she would get the lead role, but you never knew for *sure*. You never knew if no matter how good Nessa was, that they'd go for the "pretty, stick-thin girl" as the lead and the "big and talented girl" for the funny mom. But it was Nessa's voice that was so big that, in a just world, nobody could deny it. Plus, she was going to *rock* that librarian costume. She'd look *so* cute.

Nessa looked over at Lara Alexander, who had come back to school that day, and couldn't help but feel a little good that Lara was disappointed with her part. At callbacks, the role of Marian had been between Nessa and Lara, and girls like Lara got so many other things. This belonged to Nessa.

Did thinking that make Nessa a horrible person?

Nessa went over to Lara, and even though Nessa hadn't said anything mean out loud, she tried to make up for her own nasty thoughts.

"Lara, you're going to be hi-*lar*-ious in your part. I can't *wait* to see you do it. Oh my gosh, the audience is going to go bananas."

Lara smiled, and that was good.

And Nessa smiled, too, because both their names were on the only list that mattered.

Behind her, Nessa heard a group of boys' voices.

"I have to *kiss* her," one voice complained.

Brody. Brody Dixon. He'd gotten the other lead, the part of Harold Hill, the guy she had to fall in love with.

Look, she wanted to say, *I'm not so thrilled about it, either, slimeball.*

The other boys laughed. "Dude, I'm so sorry."

Was that Caleb? Caleb Rhines? What a traitor. She always helped him in jazz band when he lost his spot in the music.

Brody must have known she could hear him. Right? Who would say something like that when they knew people could hear? Nessa turned to look right at him.

Brody met her stare and strolled up to her, acting like he'd said nothing. He smiled his symmetrical smile and put a hand on her shoulder. She tried not to grimace.

"We're going to be amazing," he said to her.

He waited, as if she was supposed to smile or giggle or bat her lashes in response. Nessa raised an eyebrow at him. "We'll see."

His grin stayed plastered on his face as he added, "It was

really nice of Mr. Rhodes to choose you for the part. He's such a good guy, right? You'll be great."

What in the world was that supposed to mean?

Brody walked back toward his friends, and they laughed about something—maybe her—as they headed toward the school's front doors to leave.

"You think my dad is gonna waste his time at a 'community meeting' tonight?" Nessa heard Brody joke as he led his boys off.

"*It was really nice*" to choose her? It wasn't "*nice*"! She had *earned* it! Brody got his part because he was handsome in that actory way. The boy couldn't sing his way out of a paper bag! Good thing most of the Harold Hill songs were talky and he could fake his way through them!

Oh man, was she angry.

Nessa tried to think of what her mom liked to say. *Find your center.* Her mom's center was probably Jesus. But for Nessa, it was some other feeling, some other strength within her that she didn't have a name for yet and only felt when she sang.

Find your center, Nessa.

No luck.

Mr. Rhodes was a "good guy" for casting her? *What*?

Why did she have to exist in a school with boys like Brody

in it? And why did his ridiculous opinions have to gnaw at her so relentlessly? Maybe it was because she worried that his opinion mattered the most. If not to her, then still to the rest of the school. The world.

She wanted to scream, but instead she texted Eve.

Got the part! ☺

Then she took a breath, made her face match the smiley emoji she'd just sent, and turned to the other theater kids, ready to celebrate and to pretend that nothing ever hurt.

11

SOPHIE

As her feet slammed against the dirt of the track, an electric shot of pain ricocheted from her heels to the back of her knees. But the pain didn't matter. It felt good to move so fast.

Just keep running, she told herself. *Beat your time. Win.* Her legs pulled her ahead of every other kid on the track.

There must be proof somewhere that Eve Hoffman created the list. Evidence. Or maybe Sophie didn't even need that. Maybe she just needed to start a rumor that Eve wrote it. Everyone would turn on little Eve Hoffman and think, "Of course some freak put Sophie Kane as number two so they could be number one. Because Sophie Kane is obviously number one. And everyone wants to be Sophie."

Yes, a little whisper in the right gossipy ear could end Eve.

Sophie felt herself sprinting so fast across the track that her feet hardly touched the ground. The chilly air sliced at her cheeks. Soon it would be too cold to run outdoors and they'd have to move to the indoor track.

But what if she got in trouble for spreading lies? Could she get kicked out of school for that? Expulsion might not ruin the life of someone like Eve, who could just switch to a private school or something, but it would make everything Sophie's mom had done for her pointless.

As Sophie made her way to the end of the track, the coach, Ms. Meijer, greeted her with "Good time today, kid."

The rest of the girls, one by one, headed back to the locker rooms.

"Thanks." Sophie jogged in place. "I'm gonna go again."

Ms. Meijer looked to her watch and then up at the sky, like she needed to see the sun to double-check the time. "Only once more, 'kay? That parent-student meeting starts soon."

Sophie nodded and took off.

Her torso steamed hot as she pushed herself even faster.

Just keep running.

Her mom couldn't come to the meeting, of course. Work.

Their neighbor on the fourth floor watched Bella on the days Sophie had track. So Bella was fine. Sophie could stay for the assembly if she wanted. Should she? All her friends would be there.

But were they really her friends? Could Sophie say to Amina or Hayley, "I'm mad I'm not number one? I'm angry? Let's talk about it?" Like friends do on TV, having those touchy-feely moments that end in a group hug?

No. No way. They talked about sports, boys, and videos they'd watched online. They shared selfies. Her "friends" hadn't even been over to her place. Her mom refused it. She told Sophie that "those kind of kids" would judge her. And Sophie didn't really want them there, anyway.

In her peripheral vision, she caught a group of seventh graders sitting in the bleachers, giggling in their puffy coats. She almost never saw kids sitting out there. The kids who mattered, the ones she didn't want seeing her with her makeup sweating off, had other sports practice at the same time.

Were the seventh graders laughing at her?

She should have just let Brody kiss her last week.

It had been her second time at his house. They studied with the door open, just like his dad always told them to. But when his dad went downstairs, Brody smushed up his lips and moved toward her. And Sophie wondered if he'd ever kissed someone before, because she hadn't, and she shivered at the way his lips were a little wet, like she'd be kissing spit, and she didn't want her first kiss to be like that, and so she'd jumped up, grabbed her books, and yelled, "Gotta be getting home!" like a total weirdo. They hadn't even texted about it after, in a joking way or anything.

Yes, she should've just kissed him back. Then maybe he wouldn't be asking the new number one to the dance.

Sophie slowed down at the track's end and felt her legs pulse as she came to a stop.

"Even better time." Ms. Meijer held up her stopwatch.

Sophie nodded, panting, and headed toward the shower. "Hey, Sophie, new shoes next week, okay?" she yelled out behind her. This was an every-other-week refrain from Ms. Meijer. "Seriously, you're going to hurt yourself. You've got no support down there. Come on."

"Next week, I swear!" Sophie hollered back without looking.

These shoes had lasted her a year, and they'd last her another if they had to. She wasn't going to add sneakers to her mom's list of things needed.

Sophie jumped into the shower and stayed there under the hot water until she felt sure every other girl had gone. Then she whipped out her makeup bag, made herself presentable, and swept her wet hair up into a ballerina bun. She headed toward the auditorium, taking the long way. She didn't want to bump into anybody.

What would all the parents say at the meeting? What would Principal Yu do? What *could* they do?

When Sophie opened the door to the stairwell, she felt relief at the low lighting and silence. If she'd spoken, her voice would have echoed.

And then Sophie did hear an echo, an airy but grating voice that bounced up the stairwell. And it was talking about her.

12

EVE

Text message, after school, unknown number, obviously Miranda Garland:

u didnt tell me the little hand necklaces are a jewish thing? i just googled it when someone said something (thanks for the rec btw lots of compliments on it today!) wow weird haha no but srsly I had no idea u were jewish cuz your soooo pretty. wanna go to the mall w me and bree this wknd? itll be fun ill text u

Text message, after school, another unknown number:

i gotta be honest youd be a lot cuter if you plucked your eyebrows. ur kinda hairy.

Text message, another unknown number:

how many ppl have u kissed??????

13

SOPHIE

"She's always been that kind of pretty that's only pretty because she does everything right, you know?" Hayley Salem rasped.

"Totally," Liv answered.

"She knows how to 'look' pretty," Hayley said. "Not *be* pretty. I mean, have you ever seen her without makeup?"

"No. Have you?"

"No."

"And actually," another voice said. Amina. Who, all the way back in sixth grade, had sat by Sophie in homeroom, painfully shy but sweet and stunning, and who Sophie had seen potential in. "Eve Hoffman is beautiful in the way Sophie's not. Like, that natural way. Like, in those pictures of celebrities without makeup, some look disgusting and some look even better? Eve's the even better."

"And Sophie's the disgusting," Hayley giggled.

"No, no," Amina defended her. "She's cute and you know it. She's just . . . overrated, I guess? In the school?"

"Agreed," Liv concurred.

"Agreed," Hayley parroted.

"And you know who's also pretty? Rose. I know she's kind of annoying, but she looks like a mermaid or something," Liv said.

"Oh my gosh, she totally does! Or, wait, is it just the flowy-red-hair thing?" Hayley continued as they opened the door to the first floor.

Sophie held her breath at the top of the staircase. She waited until the door on the first floor had shut behind them, and she used her runner's legs to speed down into the emptiest, darkest room in school she could find. And there she hid, like a mouse in the wall.

14

EVE

Text message, as her family drove into the school parking lot, unknown number:

u there?

hey its brody

u think about what i asked?

What should she do? What should she say? How should she act? Complimented? As afraid as she really felt?

Eve prayed she didn't see Brody at the assembly. She didn't want to see *anyone*. There, in the school auditorium, kids who hid behind those unknown numbers would surround her. And they'd continue sizing her up.

Eve's parents had refused to leave her at home with Abe. They said she had to "join her community." At this, Abe had rolled his eyes.

"Sorry, man." Abe put a hand on her shoulder. "And what if your own community has turned on you, huh?" he added to himself as he headed to his room. "What then, Mom and Dad . . ."

The assembly was packed. Eve found herself looking at every eighth grader and wondering which of them had sent her which text. She wore a baggy hoodie to hide inside, and she turned her phone off because she couldn't take any more buzzing.

Apparently Principal Yu had emailed Eve's parents about getting Eve in to see the school counselor. But Eve told them she was fine. So far, thank goodness, they believed it. Hopefully they could get out of there before Principal Yu had a chance to grab her parents and persuade them to make Eve talk to someone.

Nessa and her parents found Eve and hers, and Nessa filled her in on the entire cast list. They did their special handshake, a series of seven moves.

"I knew you'd get the part." Eve smiled.

"Well, yeah." Nessa pretended to pose with a microphone like a pop star. "But, ew, Brody my-dad-ran-for-Senate-one-time Dixon got Harold Hill."

Should Eve tell Nessa about Brody's invitation to the dance? She'd kept it to herself all day.

Before Eve could decide whether to say anything or not, Principal Yu came to the stage to speak.

Eve saw that Curtis Milford sat a few rows to the left of them, and she made sure to keep her face pointed toward the right so he couldn't even try to catch her attention.

As Principal Yu began to speak, several parents' hands shot up.

Despite Principal Yu's attempts to assure the parents they'd have a chance to talk, some moms and dads stood up one by one in order to yell, first at Principal Yu and then at one another.

Eve took out her notebook and buried her face inside it. She continued the poem she'd left unfinished yesterday morning. Words and images drowned out the voices around her.

"I just hope this doesn't start some kind of witch hunt in the school," one of the standing dads said. "Like every boy here is a suspect. Look, we all did this kind of stuff when we were kids. It's normal."

"Oh, 'boys will be boys,' right?" a mom hollered at him. Hayley Salem sat next to her. They shared the same nearly translucent skin and hair.

"Oh, like girls can't be cruel, too," another mom chimed in.

"And do girls grow up to do the same things we see boys doing?" Hayley's mom continued. "Do girls grow up to hurt other girls the way the boys do? Have you *watched the news recently*?"

Speaking over the agitated parents, Principal Yu repeated her whole spiel from the other day about the counselors, how they'd find the kid who did it, how bullying would not be tolerated, and on and on, but the blaring symphony of anger grew louder.

Eve kept writing.

"This is kinda exciting!" Nessa whispered to Eve. "Oh man, Lara's parents look so mad," she added.

"I heard she might drop out of this school and transfer to Greenmount," said a voice behind them.

They turned around and saw Amina Alvi's exquisite face, framed by her wavy, almost-black hair. Eve saw that Amina's mom, sitting next to her, shared that perfect face, though hers was framed by a hijab decorated with bright orange and pink swirls.

But why did Eve notice how pretty Amina was? She knew nothing about Amina except that she thought Amina was pretty. Maybe Eve was just as bad as whoever wrote the list.

"She must be so upset," Amina whispered. "And Greenmount

may be a private school, but do you think that means they're nicer? *Pssh*. I doubt it."

Amina's dad put a finger to his lips, and Amina leaned back in her chair. Then she shook her head and gave Eve a look that said, "Parents, right?" Eve hadn't spoken to Amina since fifth grade. And she was a Sophie. This was all so strange.

Eve turned back to her paper, scribbling as fast as she could, the thoughts tumbling out in a ramble.

"Lara better not leave the school. She's got a good part in the show!" Nessa murmured, though Eve was hardly listening.

Try as she might to shut out the yelling, snippets of arguments continued to jump out at her:

". . . the tech-age version of graffiti on the bathroom walls!"

"Don't twist my words!"

". . . impossible to reason with you people."

"Do we really need to turn this into some kind of drama?"

". . . nobody meaner than a middle school girl."

"There are other options than *this* school, you know . . ."

"Not everyone *has* those options!"

And on and on.

Principal Yu said something about "meaningful dialogue," and Eve heard her dad scoff.

Then another woman stood up, and the clear bell of her voice seemed to take over the room.

"I think we need to hear from the children," she said. "How do *they* feel about this?"

Eve lowered her head farther into her notebook.

"I notice that most of the children here today are girls. Understandable. Me, I came with my son."

Eve could hear the rustle of her classmates looking over shoulders to investigate which boy came with this mom. Even Eve looked up.

Beside the woman, his head hanging as low to the floor as Eve's, sat Winston Byrd, the quiet Brody guy.

"I propose that our sons need this assembly most of all. Look, these girls have been made to feel less than human," she went on.

Eve remembered her brother saying the same thing.

Winston's mom stood tall, her demeanor confident, as if she did this all the time. "To not be on the list, you're getting the message that you're ugly. And in our world, where from the age of one a girl's looks are treated as all-important, a girl being perceived as 'ugly' sends her the message that she has less *value*. And for those on the list, they're being told that their purpose is to be looked at. Ranked. The poor girl sitting at number one . . . How does *she* feel?"

Eve felt her mom stiffen at the same time that she did. No one would make Eve talk, would they?

"Our boys need to hear this. They need to begin to understand their classmates' pain. I mean, in this context, being number ten, five, or one is not a *compliment*, okay, girls? Okay, *boys*?"

"Better than the alternative," her dad grunted as her mom lightly hit his arm.

"Dad, stop it." Eve may have whispered aloud, or maybe she just thought it. What did *he* know about being a girl?

"I think we should hear from each of these girls," Winston's mom continued. "Let's give them a voice. Boys, listen. Girls . . . speak."

Eve stopped hearing her. Would they start with number one and go in order? How could she escape?

Winston's mom made a lot of sense, and Eve agreed with what she was saying, but Eve had never asked to be number one. She certainly never asked to be the spokesperson for this lady's point of view.

"I gotta go," Eve whispered to her mom and Nessa, and she stumbled over the laps in her row, dropping some loose papers from her notebook as she went, but not stopping to consider them. She had to leave.

She ran out the door, searching for whatever other room lay nearest to her, where she could hide.

"Hey!" Eve heard a boy's voice behind her, but she ignored it. "Hey, wait!"

The choir room. Right down the hall.

She pulled open the anchor-heavy doors and let them clamp shut behind her, escaping the voice. She was done hearing from boys right then.

She put her back against the door by the wall and let herself slide to the floor.

The tears came. Rushing out seemingly without end, like the text messages she'd been getting all day.

And as the tears poured, she heard the creak of a choir chair from somewhere in the darkness beyond her.

"Who's there?" Eve spoke to the shadows.

The shadows spoke back: "Well, isn't this just perfect."

"I'll go." Eve turned to push the door.

"Who do you think you are?" the voice called to her.

Eve glanced back to see a figure emerge from the depths of the choir room, where the tall kids always sat. And there, with her arms crossed and a sour glare on her face, stood Sophie Kane.

"You've been here for the whole assembly?" Eve managed to squeak out.

"I've been here long enough to hear you freak out, let's just say that," Sophie answered, looking Eve up and down the way Brody had in the hallway the morning the list came out. "Of all people, of course it's you." Sophie stormed toward her. "*You* . . ."

Eve had never been in a fight before. Was Sophie going to slap her? Should she run? Why couldn't her legs move?

"You think you can get away with this?" Sophie hissed, getting closer and closer.

What was Sophie Kane talking about?

"Oh wow." Sophie laughed a frightening laugh. Like a supervillain. "You little . . ."

"I'm . . . sorry?" Eve didn't know what she was sorry for, though.

"Do you have any *idea* what you've done to my life?" Sophie ran a spastic hand through her hair.

"Me?" Eve's jaw dropped.

"Yes, *you*."

"What are you talking about?"

But before Sophie could answer, they heard the door begin to open.

Eve and Sophie froze, catching each other's eye.

It was the first time Eve had actually looked Sophie Kane directly in the face. Sophie's eyes were as dark blue as morning glories, and she was perfectly tan, even in October.

Wait. Was that a fake tan?

Here Eve was, thinking about a girl's looks again.

"Don't come in!" Sophie ordered.

As Nessa entered, Sophie scurried toward the back of the room.

Nessa slammed the door shut behind her. "Oh man. You've been crying. Look, don't listen to that lady. She's got some of the girls talking about their feelings now, so it's gonna go on all night." Nessa wrapped an arm around Eve.

Eve felt the tears stirring inside her again. "I had to get out of there."

"I know," Nessa comforted her.

A loud sigh came from the chairs.

"Is . . . ," Nessa said as she separated from Eve, "someone in here?"

Eve nodded in Sophie's direction.

"Can we put some chairs in front of the door or something?" Sophie complained from where she sat. "Is there a lock? How do we stop the whole frickin' school from barging in here?"

"What are *you* doing here?" Nessa turned to Sophie. "Shouldn't you be with your minions?"

"What are *you* doing here? Shouldn't you be talking about your feelings with Principal Yu?" Sophie shot back.

"I'm making sure my best friend is okay!" Nessa pulled Eve in tighter.

"Okay?" Sophie stood up again. She seemed to tower over them, even from far away. "O*kay*? No one is okay, thanks to her." She pointed her finger right at Eve as if she were putting a curse on her.

"*Me*?" Eve took a step toward Sophie.

"Yes, you. Of course *you're* okay. You're the new *Thing*." Sophie shook her head. "Unbelievable."

"*What*?" Eve's gut spoke for her.

"Don't play stupid with me, Snow White," Sophie Kane roared. "I know you wrote the list yourself. Soon everyone will know."

Nessa jumped to her defense with "She didn't—" but Eve surprised herself by cutting Nessa off and speaking all on her own.

"You think I'm 'okay'? You think I *want* people telling me I stuff my bra? You think I *like* it when someone texts me 'you're kinda hairy'? Like, *what*?!"

"Geez, Evie, I didn't know . . . ," Nessa broke in.

"Why do you think I dress this way, huh?" She motioned to her brother's hoodie. "You think I *want* to be looked at?"

Even more tears rose back up and leaked out, down her face and onto the front of her clothes. "You think I don't know this was never supposed to happen?" She tried to hold in a sob, but it forced itself out, anyway. "You think I think I'm some supermodel or something? It's obviously some cruel joke." Eve wiped her eyes. "Just please, tell all your friends to leave me *alone*!"

And then the only sounds in the room were Eve's cries and the light pats of Nessa's palm on Eve's back, until Sophie groaned.

"Okay, so you're trying to say you didn't put that Post-it on my back?" Sophie jutted a hip out, and her arms guarded her chest once again.

"What? I was trying to get it *off* you!" Eve threw her hands up in the air. "What is even happening?" She turned to Nessa. "Let's just go. Please."

"You're right." Nessa shook her head at Sophie. "She's just like the rest of them."

"I'm not!"

At Sophie's words, Eve and Nessa stopped.

"Just wait. Let's say I believe you and you didn't write it." She looked from Nessa to Eve and back. "Who did, then?"

The three of them stood in silence.

Eve had no idea who wrote the list, but whoever it was, she could feel them with her now, always. It was someone who had looked at her too much. Maybe someone who wanted to mock her. And not just her, but the girls left off the list, too. Someone who didn't care about their feelings, or about how a number could dissolve into a girl's skin like ink and never leave.

"I don't know," Eve said at the same time as Nessa began to name names.

"It could be a girl." Nessa angled herself against the door. "I've wondered that. Hayley Salem?"

Sophie nodded. "Yeah, yeah, for sure, that's what I've been saying! A girl!" She walked to the piano and leaned against it.

"And, yeah, probably someone in the top ten." Nessa took a step toward Sophie. "Someone who would get something out of it, right?"

"But Hayley Salem would make herself number one." Sophie shook her head at the thought. "She's too stupid. She'd make it obvious. She wouldn't put herself as five. And why would any of them put Eve at the top of the list?"

"Yeah, good point." Nessa moved farther inside the room, inching closer toward Sophie at the piano. "And a girl who just wants attention doesn't get much out of a list that gives *Evie* all the attention, right?" she theorized.

"Why would anyone want this kind of attention? Maybe it's someone who hates me," Eve muttered, moving away from the door, to stand beside Nessa.

"So who hates you, then?" Sophie asked, her expression skeptical.

"Well, did *you* write the list?" Nessa mimicked Sophie's hip-out stance. "Because you sure seem to hate her!"

Sophie rolled her eyes. "No, I'm serious. Who hates you?"

"I don't know." Eve pictured each unknown number that had texted her and tried to match a face with the numbers and messages.

"Weird." Sophie sighed. "Well, maybe you're just a random name, and the whole point was to get at me. Lots of people hate *me*."

Was that pride Eve detected in her voice?

Nessa laughed. "Oh yeah, says the most popular girl in school."

"Um, excuse me? Don't you know that 'most popular' and 'most hated' go together?"

She wasn't wrong, Eve realized. Weren't she and Nessa always looking down on Sophie and Brody and their friends? Didn't everyone assume they were snobby and fake?

"Yeah, I mean, think about Brody Dixon," Nessa said, echoing Eve's thoughts. "He's literally the last person I want to do this show with." Nessa took a sharp inhale. "Wait." She gasped again, and her hands fluttered in the air like she was trying to grasp onto something. "Wait, that's it!"

"Oh my God." Sophie put her hand over her mouth.

"Of course!" Nessa laughed. She walked up to Sophie, stopping inches apart from her. "Duh!"

"Of course." Sophie smacked the top of the piano. "Of *course*!" she repeated.

"*What*?" Eve hurried after Nessa. "You think it's Brody?"

"Who *else* would it be?" Nessa brought out her phone and pulled up the list, the light of the screen creating a glow around her.

"Do you think it's him alone or with his friends?" Sophie leaned in toward Nessa, ignoring Eve.

"Who knows?" Nessa answered. "But you *know* he put them up to it even if it was his goons. Let's check the list. I bet all the girls not in the top fifty are people Brody made fun of at some point. Like me. This is the kind of list a straight-up bully makes. A jerk. A jerk who never really gets in trouble for anything he does."

Brody had made fun of Nessa in elementary school, Eve remembered. But not in a long time. Right?

"Wait." Sophie lifted a hand as if to stop the proceedings. "Wait, wait, wait, wait. Why would he do this to *me*, though?" She broke away from them to go pace by the chairs. "He asked me over to his house twice! I mean, I can show you!" She waved the phone at them. "He was basically acting like we went out. I'm sure you two know that."

Eve hadn't heard that at all, actually.

"So why would he put me as number two? It's not like I *did* anything! I just—" Sophie stopped midsentence and froze.

A moment of silence passed between them.

"Is she okay?" Nessa whispered to Eve.

"Oh," Sophie said in a softer voice, her eyes elsewhere, toward the piano pedals and then to the ceiling. A light shake of the head and then: "Never mind."

"You okay?" Nessa asked.

"Yeah. I just understand something now." Sophie flipped around to speak to Eve. "Eve, he asked you to the Halloween dance, yes?"

"Um, yeah," Eve admitted.

Nessa turned to her. "Really? Why didn't you tell me?"

Before Eve could answer, Sophie continued. She spoke like a lawyer, question after question. "What was he acting like when he asked you?"

"Um . . . nice?" Eve looked to Nessa for help, but Nessa said nothing. "I mean, I don't know, no one has ever asked me anything like that before."

"Come on, did it seem like he liked you?"

Eve thought of Brody Dixon's face that day as he'd invited her to go to the Halloween dance with him. The whole time she'd wanted to open the locker behind her and cram herself into it as the most awkward moment of her life unfolded. But when she did meet his eye, he looked . . . normal? Honest? Kind of sweet?

"Well, I don't know . . . ," Eve began.

"Come *on*," Sophie repeated. "What did he say? Tell me."

Eve told her how Brody had said they'd have a lot of fun at the dance, how it didn't have to be a big deal, how it was a shame they never talked, and how people didn't talk to one another because of these stupid separate groups everybody was stuck in. Then he told her it was no pressure and she could just think about it.

What Eve didn't say was that she'd never wanted to go out with anyone in her life—that was for girls like, well, Sophie Kane—but the only somewhat-okay part of that horrible day had been when Brody Dixon had looked her in the eye and said, "No pressure." Even now, thinking of those words let her exhale.

"Wait, wait, wait." Sophie nearly sprinted back to where Nessa stood. "Did you hear that?"

"Yeah." Nessa nodded. "'Stupid separate groups.'"

"Explain?" Eve moved to sit on the piano bench.

Nessa sat beside her. "Brody probably actually likes you."

Sophie sighed a loud, long sigh.

"And he put you as number one," Nessa went on, "because otherwise—"

"He couldn't ask you to the dance if you were a nobody." Sophie surprised Eve by sliding in on her other side.

Were they not enemies now?

"And," Sophie added, "I think he wanted a replacement. For me."

All Eve could say was "Oh."

They sat so close that Eve could smell the school shampoo on Sophie Kane's hair.

"It all checks out now." Sophie spoke in a low whisper. "That's why you're number one, and I'm number two . . ." She looked as if she were attempting to work out a math problem in her head. "He's auditioning his next girl. And trying to hurt me while he does it."

"But why would he want to hurt you?" Nessa asked, leaning over Eve toward Sophie.

"It doesn't matter," Sophie muttered.

For a moment, the three of them sat quietly. A loud truck went by outside.

And then Sophie slammed a fist on the piano keys and Eve and Nessa jumped.

"Whoa!" Nessa looked toward the door as if someone might hear them and come in.

"He can't treat people like this!" Sophie's voice escalated to a low growl. "Did you know he lives in one of the biggest houses in Glisgold?" Her leg began to bounce as if she'd had too much pop. "He has a game room. And three TVs. Maybe more, actually. His dad's bedroom? I mean, it's like its own house. Oh, and he has a dog room! A room where the dog sleeps! And Brody gets *everything* he wants. And you should hear the way he talks about girls." Sophie scooted in closer to Eve on the bench, speaking in a near whisper now, as if the worst parts about Brody were a secret. "It's like if a girl isn't pretty—"

"By *his* standards," Nessa interjected.

"Exactly. If a girl isn't pretty in his opinion, she's just a waste of time. Unless she's good at homework or something and he's on a group project with her." Sophie put a hand to her heart. "Oh my God, is that why he asked me to study? No. No. It couldn't be that."

Eve reflexively shook her head to signal "No, of course

not," but she didn't quite know what Sophie was referring to. Brody sounded so much crueler than the boy who'd spoken to her earlier that day. But still, she didn't forget the Brody of fifth grade, who had once taken her favorite book and thrown it in the mud.

"The thing is," Sophie went on, "it's not like he's not smart. He is, kind of, but only in that way where your parents have helped you with homework your whole life. And he's always giving attention to one of my friends one week, and another the next. Yeah, it's been me recently, but maybe he's changed his mind again. It was Amina before me! He's really . . . He *is* a jerk. You know what?" Sophie declared. "I *despise* him."

"Well." Nessa strummed her nails on the top of the piano. "I agree! Evie, do you remember how he constantly called the one boy in fifth grade dance class 'twinkle toes'?"

"He was a classic bully back in elementary school," Eve told Sophie, who had only come to their school in the middle of sixth grade. "Like out of a bad movie."

He never got in trouble, though. Eve remembered that part well.

"Not just elementary school," Nessa said. "He made a joke about Erin O'Brien's wheelchair last year, do you remember? Before the show he said, 'I heard about Special Olympics but never Special Broadway.'"

"Gross," Sophie murmured.

"Yeah!" Nessa nearly hollered. "A little more than 'gross'!" She put on her theater-trivia voice and continued, "Also, has he not even *heard* of Ali Stroker, the Tony Award–winning Broadway actress who happens to use a wheelchair? Like, he's not just mean and macho or whatever, he's *ignorant*!" Nessa paused. "I wish I had brought that up when he said it. I didn't say anything."

"Yeah," Eve agreed. "Me either." Why hadn't she said something? Why hadn't she remembered that until now?

"He has made every single girl in this school feel horrible," Sophie said slowly and deliberately. "He can't keep doing it."

"But what do *we* do?" Nessa asked.

"Yeah." Eve shrugged. "What *can* we do?"

"Are you kidding?" Sophie turned to them both, a gleam in her angry eye. "We get justice."

15

SOPHIE

“So what’s your plan?” Nessa asked her.

Right to the point. Sophie liked that.

“Wait,” Eve broke in. “The adults back there . . . they’re trying to work it out. If it’s Brody, they’ll handle it.”

Sophie couldn’t stop herself from muttering “Snow White” under her breath. Nessa jumped in.

“Evie,” Nessa said as they all stood up and faced one another in a triangle under the dim lights. “Did you hear those adults out there? They have no idea what our lives are actually like. And they are a mess! Just bickering among themselves.”

"Exactly!" Sophie jumped in. This Nessa girl saw the situation for what it was.

"And Brody Dixon can't go around making people cry in choir rooms," Nessa continued. "Choir rooms are for the majesty of song. For joy! This sucks, what he did."

"I'm gonna ignore that you just said 'majesty of song,'" Sophie had to say.

"You're right," Eve relented. "I just want this to go away."

"Good." Sophie felt herself begin to focus. "Because we'll need you. Before we can get justice, we'll need proof he did it. Here's our strategy."

Like she did when she led school projects, or led the Sophies, she made the decisions and gave assignments. They needed hard evidence, so Eve's job was to make Brody think she really liked him back, to get him vulnerable, and then maybe get his phone password, or look on his laptop, or ideally even ask him sweetly about the list and record his answer. Then they'd bring the confession to Principal Yu. But to achieve this, Eve would need a total makeover. He may have wanted Eve as number one, but she needed to *act* like number one if Brody Dixon was going to go out with her long enough for them to catch him. Sophie understood this, even if Eve didn't.

And Sophie was obviously the expert in how to look like number one, so she'd teach her.

"And then I can get my old life back?" Eve Hoffman asked her.

"Sure," Sophie said. What was her old life, anyway?

"But you'll have to be the actress for a little while," Nessa told Eve with a grim expression on her face.

"I'll be at your house this weekend," Sophie decreed. "I'll text you."

"I'll create a group text. I'll call it"—Nessa paused for dramatic effect—"the Choir Room Trio."

Sophie grimaced at the name, but she moved on.

She declared that Nessa could use her position as the other lead in *The Music Man* to watch for any whispered bragging about the list and any signs of weakness. As for Sophie, well, she was the captain. She'd manage the plans and, in the meantime, welcome Eve into the Sophies. The task was enormous. But she'd make it happen.

They heard a commotion in the hall. Assembly was ending.

"Let's get justice." Sophie made a beeline toward the exit.

"Justice," the two other girls repeated.

Sophie threw the doors open and headed off.

Justice. Sure. There was justice involved. The justice of her being back in her rightful place as number one. The place she'd earned. Did little Eve Hoffman deserve to be there? Not a chance.

As the bus rolled down Greer Road in the rapidly darkening evening, she pressed her forehead to the glass of the window and watched the landscape of Glisgold go by. Police department, fire department, Santa Maria Parish, Harmony Chapel, a big sign that read WE ALL SIN, JESUS SAVES, two McDonald's restaurants, and a couple of outlets. The bus flew by her mom's diner, and Sophie tried to catch her mom's silhouette in the windows' reflection, but all she could make out were groupings of families, warm and seated, probably waiting for her mom to bring them a meal.

She wondered if Brody Dixon's dad had ever eaten at the diner and ordered a meal from her mom. She wondered if Brody had been there, too.

He really was a jerk. If she could talk to her mom about this, her mom would say Brody was just like her dad. Not that her dad was rich, or was used to things going his way, but he *wanted* things to go his way, and that was what he cared about most. And her mom said that, for her dad, if things weren't going his way, he just left. Like how he'd been tired of Glisgold and had given up his job in town and taken up a touring gig playing bass for his old band. She'd never forget the fight her mom and dad had, going on two years ago now, as he packed his bags. He came every few weeks, for holidays and stuff, but less and less.

And she'd never forget the way Brody had pretended to laugh it off when she hadn't kissed him back, but how he'd been planning something awful.

The bus neared the edge of town. As an old lady stepped off it, carrying several tote bags filled to the brim with who knows what, she gave Sophie a stare of concern, maybe, or disapproval. Sophie looked away.

She used to think of Brody as just . . . the boy who came with being at the top. Like the nude heels that go with a mint green dress. But maybe there were other options. Something funky or Christmasy, like red flats—a random boy in the school who no one expected she'd be with.

She certainly didn't want *him* anymore.

Or even her "friends," whose words—*I mean, have you ever seen her without makeup?*—echoed in her memory.

Sophie couldn't wait to get home to Bella.

She leaned her head against the icy cold window, sleep overtaking her, only to wake up mere moments before the bus passed Silver Ledge. She threw her backpack on and hopped off the bus and into the apartment building, where Bella lay asleep in front of Mrs. Jackson's TV, Cheetos crumbs all over her purple sweater.

Sophie thanked Mrs. Jackson and took Bella back to their apartment for bed.

She tried to focus on her homework, but those Spanish verbs still wouldn't stick, and the math swirled in her brain. In the past, she'd always been so good at all of this. Had being number one been a lie in other ways, too? Was she less smart than she thought? Was school getting too hard for her?

Sophie dropped her pen and paper and went to stand in front of the full-length mirror.

Her eyelids sagged from trying to stay up on her mom's late shift nights to see her. Her hair, out of its ballerina bun, lay damp and limp on her shoulders, looking as tired as she was. The highlights she'd done with a box of hair dye had begun to fade from daffodil yellow to dead autumn grass. She puckered a few times in the mirror. Her lips were just too, too thin. Maybe one day she'd buy that collagen-infused lip gloss that supposedly made your lips plumper. One day, when she was rich enough to buy her mom a house in California on the beach, and get massages every day from a personal masseuse, and get her nails done every week with Bella . . .

Sophie put on her headphones, applied her mom's red lipstick, and lip-synched into the mirror. This was always when she felt the prettiest, when she pretended to be someone else.

Maybe tonight wasn't a night to finish her homework.

What did it matter, anymore, now that, for the time being, everyone at school would look at her like she was "less than" Eve Hoffman?

Sophie wiped off the lipstick.

Maybe she didn't even need to wear it tomorrow. Who cared, anyway, if everyone was looking at her differently already?

No. No, she couldn't. She wouldn't be herself without it. Plus, like Liv, Hayley, and Amina had said, the lipstick was what made her so pretty.

Soon, after they exposed Brody and the list stopped mattering, and all anyone cared about was the drama of Brody Dixon's downfall and Sophie Kane's detective work and fight for justice, Sophie would eclipse Eve Hoffman and take back her rightful place at the top.

For now, Sophie collapsed into bed to the dependable drone of her sister's snores.

16

EVE

"Hey." Abe cracked open Eve's door later that night.

Eve lay in bed watching her and Nessa's favorite reality show, *Dance House*, in which a bunch of dancers live in a house together while they audition for some big dance scholarship. Each week another dancer gets cut. Eve and Nessa texted throughout all of it every week.

One sec, she wrote to Nessa before looking at Abe. "What's up?" she asked her brother.

"So how'd it go?" He walked in and leaned against her bookshelf.

"Okay, I guess," she lied.

"And what the heck are you watching?" he asked as one dancer tried to pull the other one to the ground by her ponytail.

"Oh, nothing." Eve turned the laptop away.

Abe came over to sit on the edge of her bed. "This list thing absolutely blows, doesn't it?"

"It hasn't been the best week." Eve shrugged.

"Middle school is the worst," he said. "You're gonna love high school."

"Yeah?"

"Yeah, everyone is older and, like, chills out a little bit."

"Cool."

"And at Rockson they have the best English teacher: Mr. Melby. He's this dude with Albert Einstein hair who's always quoting Shakespeare and stuff. You'd go nuts for him."

"That sounds awesome." Eve grinned.

"I'm just saying, one year and you'll be out of Ford."

If she could even last the year! "Yeah, I know," she told him.

But that didn't change the fact that she had to go back to school tomorrow, and be stared at, and pretend to like Brody Dixon, and let Sophie do some weird makeover on her that weekend, and just pray things went back to normal after it was all over.

"I understand your skepticism," Abe said. "Just don't let this crap change you, okay?"

It felt odd to have Abe speak to her this way, because she didn't know what about her he thought might change. *He* was the one who had changed. They used to race their bicycles in the park and build legendary forts out of shelves and blankets where they would play Slapjack and War for hours at a time. But now he wasn't around much, and the forts were years behind them. Plus, he was always fighting with their dad about articles and books she'd never read. Sometimes it even seemed as if he *liked* making their dad angry.

She couldn't imagine changing as much as *he* had.

"I won't," she answered.

"Okay. Good." Abe headed out of her room and hollered, "Night!" as the door closed.

Eve called Nessa.

"Is this 'number one' calling? *Number one*? Oh my god." Nessa fake-hyperventilated.

"Oh, be quiet."

"Too soon? Sorry."

"Okay, so . . ." Eve turned the laptop back around. "What'd I miss?"

"Well, Teeny might get kicked out of the house for the

hair pull, but she's so talented the judges are having a hard time doing that and might give her another chance."

"'Kay." Eve snuggled under her covers to watch the final dance numbers.

"So how about that Sophie Kane, huh?" Nessa asked as one of the girls performed. "Do you trust her?"

Eve took a moment before answering. Sophie had been so angry with her, and then so certain that it was Brody mere moments later, like she just wanted someone—anyone—to blame. "I'm not sure."

The girl who was performing did a triple pirouette.

"Wow," they both said at the same time.

"*I* don't trust her," Nessa admitted. "She's smarter than I thought she'd be, though. I'll give her that. Oh my gosh, first Teeny pulls a ponytail and now she's yelling at a judge?"

"Wait, why didn't you think she was smart?" Eve pressed her. "Isn't she good in classes and stuff?"

"Yeah, I guess. But look at her."

Eve tried to remember if she'd ever assumed that Sophie was stupid. She had never really considered it, but if someone had directly asked her before that night if she thought Sophie was smart, she probably would've said no. Why?

"So do you think if I do this makeover thing that everybody

will think *I'm* stupid?" Eve asked. "Will *you* think I'm stupid? Because of how I look?"

"No! Of course not. I just mean—forget it."

A dancer fell midflip.

"OW!" both Nessa and Eve hollered, and then giggled.

They watched in silence as the judges assessed the performance.

"Hey." Eve tried to sound casual, but one thing Nessa had said earlier that night kept coming back into her head. "It seems like you *really* hate Brody."

"Um, *yeah*."

"He hasn't made fun of you in a long time, though, right? Like since we were kids?"

Eve heard a grunt on the other line.

"Just because I'm not sobbing about stuff all the time doesn't mean I'm not getting made fun of, okay?" Nessa answered with a sharpness Eve hadn't expected.

"Okay!" Eve backed off. "Sorry if I 'sobbed' tonight."

"No, that's not what I mean!" Nessa *argh*ed into the phone. "Well, yeah, I guess I don't tell you everything that everyone says to me sometimes. Brody's not my biggest fan. I'm not his type of girl. You don't get it."

"What? I can get it, I—I—" Eve stammered before Nessa interrupted.

"Hey—why didn't *you* tell *me* that Brody asked you to the Halloween dance? That's huge, and you didn't text me all day!"

"I'm sorry! I just . . . felt weird."

They sat in silence.

"I should finish my homework," Nessa told her, sounding far off.

"Yeah, me too."

Eve wanted to cry again. She wanted to say to Nessa, "Tell me everything that everyone says to you, and I'll come after them!" But she knew she wouldn't come after them, because that was terrifying. And she wanted to say, "I kind of liked the feeling of Brody asking me, and I couldn't tell you that," but that, too, didn't escape her lips. She felt like saying either would make Nessa angrier.

The judges huddled for their final elimination process. Teeny wept in anticipation of getting cut. She really needed that scholarship if she wanted her dance dream to come true.

"We're not in a fight, right?" Eve asked.

"No, no. Come on. We're best friends."

But instead of Teeny getting axed, the girl whose ponytail had been pulled got cut! Apparently, she had let the ponytail pull affect her final dance performance, which the judges deemed unacceptable. After Nessa and Eve ranted about the inequity of this for several minutes, they blew kisses into the phone and said good night.

Within seconds Eve's phone buzzed, and she instinctively went to pick it up, but what she saw made her drop the phone as if it were piping hot. Another boy. Another text. This one gross. So gross it was mean.

The words from the texts had begun to repeat themselves in her mind on an endless loop, like her favorite poems once did only days ago.

She wondered if Sophie got these kinds of texts. And then she wondered why, after they left the choir room, Sophie had walked toward the street in front of the school, headed toward the bus stop.

Eve turned her phone off and threw it on the carpet. With no phone, no alarm would wake her up in the morning. She'd be late. Or maybe she could just miss school altogether. Maybe she would never go back.

Maybe she was already changing.

17

NESSA

"And so," Nessa said, launching into an explanation of her life plan over family dinner a couple of days after the choir room meeting, "after I get my college degree in musical theater—"

"Wow. Now *that's* a terrible idea," her sister Delma mumbled into her plate.

"I'll easily get a couple of regional theater gigs under my belt, and then I'll have my Equity card—"

"Huh?"

Nessa sighed. "The union. The actors' union? Anyway.

Then I'll be pretty much set. If you think about it that way, it's a pretty reasonable career choice, you have to admit."

"Are you just going to let her chatter all dinner without asking me about *my* day?" Delma put her fork down and challenged their parents.

Her dad smiled. "You're right, you're right. Go ahead, Del. How was your day?"

Delma shrugged. "Fine."

"See?" Nessa hollered. "She doesn't even have anything to say!"

"It's the principle," Delma whined.

It was a miracle that Nessa's boring family—a pediatrician dad, an occupational therapist mom, and a math-whiz older sister—created a star like her.

When she took a breath to eat some of her casamiento, her dad asked her if the uproar over the list had died down at all. She told him no, which was true, at least for people who weren't her.

Nessa was determined not to let the list get to her. Because the thing was, Nessa was fabulous. She knew what happened when she walked onto a stage. The room stilled. And she heard the sound that echoed back into her ears when she sang in the shower. She had a gift. And when it came to the mirror, well, truth be told, Nessa loved looking into it. She loved the freckles her dad had given her, and the thick, black hair her mother had passed down (well, she had a love/hate relationship with her hair, but mostly love).

So what if her Dad's Irish Catholic parents in Grand Rapids told her she should focus on "eating healthier"? She ate healthy, but also not, sometimes. Just like anybody else. And it was none of their business! Especially when Gram and Gramps were pouring butter all over *everything* they touched! Geez, they'd probably put butter on sushi!

And when she visited El Salvador every other winter break to see her mom's parents, they would say the opposite. They'd say to Delma, "You're too skinny." To be honest, Nessa loved when they said that. Take that, Delma. But that wasn't the point. The point was, everyone had his or her own opinions about how other people should look, and those opinions were different all over the *world*, so how could any one opinion be true?

But, of course, no one in school cared about that. And it didn't feel *good* to have kids make fun of her for practically her whole life. It was the worst! One time, in sixth grade, two boys fought over whether she was "fat" or "chubby," like her body was a visual presentation in debate class or something.

They acted like she couldn't even hear them, pointing at her the whole time. That infuriated her. And, boy, did she let them know. And when people made jokes on TV about "fat girls" or whatever, she could feel her whole heart burn up in utter rage. She wished she could let those people know how obnoxious they were, too, just like she had to those sixth grade boys.

She could fill a book with the obnoxious things people said.

And, yes, fine, it kind of bothered her that even though *she* knew that she was super cute, no one *else* seemed to.

It bothered her a lot, actually.

But she didn't like to let people know it. Not the kids who said awful things to her, and not even Eve. Eve couldn't ever understand, anyway. Eve had it a lot easier than she realized.

Nessa's dad turned the conversation over to her. "How are you feeling about that list?" he asked, clearly pretending not to be worried.

"Whatever," she said. "You know me. I don't care about that stuff."

Her mom shook her head. "So sad," she muttered. "So cruel."

"Yeah," Nessa agreed. "Cruel."

"You're all perfect, exactly as you are. Each one of you," her mom went on, sounding like she could cry.

Nessa looked away.

"Cheers to that," her dad added.

As they cleared the table and did dishes, her dad started kissing her mom's neck and Nessa and Delma groaned.

Her mom and dad were disgusting. But kinda sweet. How could two people who were so different be so obsessed with each other? They didn't even like the same music and movies!

"What's the problem?" her dad said as he turned to them, grinning. "Your mother happens to be quite kissable."

"Oh man, it's getting vomit-worthy." Delma wiped her hands and went upstairs.

The read-through for *The Music Man* took place the next day, a Friday. The moment had arrived for her to shine, and to keep an ear and eye out for the holes in Brody Dixon's mask of innocence.

At the read-through, they just had to speak the lyrics of the songs, not sing, so Brody might actually do okay. Add a melody and he'd flounder on the floor like a fish on land.

And Nessa wasn't too annoyed with him to admit that his acting was good.

At auditions, when he'd looked at her all googly-eyed during their romance scene and professed, "I can't go . . . For the first time in my life, I got my foot caught in the door . . . ," Nessa almost *liked* Brody for a second. She peered into his baby blues and felt her insides flutter a bit. Because, like a good actor, he meant it when he said it.

Unfortunately, when the audition had ended, Brody was Brody again, which was just sad for everybody.

Good actor or no, Brody Dixon would not get away with what he'd done to the girls of Ford. Nessa would make sure of it. Of *course* he was the guilty one. Only someone like him, who thought it was "nice" of Mr. Rhodes to give her the lead role, who didn't see that she deserved it in every way, could do something as horrible as rate the girls. She couldn't think of anyone else in school with a pile of ashes in place of a heart.

Nessa was a frickin' Gryffindor. She knew she had courage. She knew she had heart. And she was going to protect her best friend, Eve Hoffman, who had definitely not figured out how awesome she was yet. And she was going to help Sophie Kane, too, because even though she didn't trust Sophie, *nobody* deserved to be treated the way all the girls had been treated.

Nessa was going to put on her cape and teach them that you need to show the world a brave face, whether you feel brave or not.

Plus, a little revenge would be nice.

18

EVE

Sophie Kane had announced she would come over on Saturday. Saturday was Shabbat, and Eve had resisted, but Sophie texted her, **This is what works for me.**

Eve relented. **Only at two, can't do earlier.** For some reason, she couldn't find it within herself to say no to Sophie Kane.

Did Eve's parents have to choose to live in a town where they were the only Jewish family? She could hear her mom's answer: "People get sick and need help everywhere. There's a perfectly fine Conservative synagogue twenty minutes away."

When her family got home from synagogue, Eve sat in the kitchen with her mom and waited for Sophie.

"Who is this girl again?" her mom asked as she brought over a bowl of apple slices to the table.

"Her name is Sophie Kane."

"She's number two!" Hannah hollered from all the way down in the TV room.

Of *course* Hannah had the list memorized.

"How can you even hear us in here?" Eve's mom shook her head but smiled. "You two have a class project? You and this Sophie Kane?"

Eve nodded, perhaps too enthusiastically.

By the time the clock read two-thirty P.M., Eve was getting nervous.

"Mom, I'm sure she texted me if she's just late or not coming. Maybe I should just turn on the phone." Sitting in the kitchen, Eve's powered-down cell phone lay plugged in next to the microwave, and she stared at it as if it could transmit information to her through telepathy.

"You know, honey, it's your choice if you want to turn it on," her mom said. "You chose to not use your cell on Shabbat. I didn't force you."

This made her feel even more guilty, because her parents were so cool about the whole thing.

What would Sophie think when Eve didn't text back? It was too hard to explain to her.

"So are you two new friends?" her mom asked.

At that moment, the doorbell rang. Eve bolted up to get it.

Sophie Kane stood in the doorway with what Eve was beginning to see was her typical pose: hand on a hip, head tilted slightly to the side, long hair resting behind her shoulders.

But what wasn't typical of Sophie Kane, at least the tiny bit of Sophie Kane that Eve knew, was that she was accompanied by a little girl.

"This is Bella, my sister."

"Bella Marie Kane!" the girl announced, in this kind of grande dame voice that old British ladies used in TV shows.

Sophie nudged Bella with a shoulder. "I had to bring her."

"It's okay." Eve opened the door and let them in.

Her mom shook both their hands and asked them if they wanted anything to eat. Sophie declined. Bella jumped up and down and said yes, and Eve's mom and Bella made up a plate of snacks and brought them to the TV room.

"I found you a friend," Eve heard her mom say to Hannah.

"Hi! Bella Marie Kane," Eve heard.

"She's in fourth grade." Sophie looked around their hallway

and living room, and Eve couldn't begin to guess at what she was thinking.

"I get it. Mine's in fifth."

When they got up to Eve's room, Sophie circled around it slowly. She reminded Eve of a lioness stalking out the perimeter of her territory.

Sophie stopped in front of Eve's music box. She lifted it up and ballet music began to play.

"My bubbe got that for me when I was, like, five," Eve said apologetically.

Sophie looked back at her as if she'd forgotten Eve was in the room. "It's really pretty."

"Thanks."

Sophie pulled a bag off her shoulder and sat down. "Let's get to work."

Out of that bag came concealers, foundations, blush, mascara, eye shadow, eyeliner, a lot of little plastic baggies the size of quarters filled with what looked like lip colors, and a whole sack of bobby pins.

"What are you going to do to me?" Eve asked.

"Teach you to make yourself as cute as you can be." Sophie arranged the makeup along the side of the bed.

Eve glanced toward her bedroom door. If her mom walked in, she'd be in shock.

"That's a little much," Eve demurred.

Sophie gave her a narrow-eyed glare. "What did you think we were doing? Hanging out? I'm going to teach you how to do a morning routine to get you looking a little less background dancer and a little more front-and-center."

Eve felt her face flush even though she didn't feel particularly embarrassed . . . why did her face do this? "But if Brody did put me on the list to make it okay to go out with me or something, then why would I need to change? Wouldn't that mean he likes me the way I look now?"

Sophie groaned and did one of her hair flips. "He won't *stay* into you if you keep wearing sports teams' shirts that don't fit. Maybe he's giving you a hint to change a little for him. I mean, seriously?"

Eve looked down at herself. That day she still wore her clothes from synagogue: a white blouse with a midcalf-length black skirt. She felt herself fingering her hamsa necklace.

Sophie looked her up and down, too. "You don't look so bad now," she said. "A little nunlike, maybe, but that's it. At least I can see your waist."

"Ha," Eve said to herself. "Definitely not a nun."

Sophie quizzically scrunched up her made-up face.

"I'm Jewish. These are my synagogue clothes."

Sophie said nothing.

For a second, Eve thought that Sophie might leave. She knew that was paranoid, but she'd heard stories, stories from her dad about a long time ago, when he was a kid. Before his family had moved to St. Louis Park, Minnesota, where there were lots of other Jewish families, he'd been beaten up one time and called "Jew boy." Her mom hadn't had that experience, but she'd long ago taught Eve that some people still thought bad things about Jews, and that sometimes people might think those things of her, and that she should always just be herself. But whenever people found out, she had that millisecond of wondering how they'd react.

It didn't help that recently, only a few towns away, a neo-Nazi group had marched in the streets.

But Sophie simply said, "So let's see more of those synagogue clothes."

Relief flooded Eve as she pulled open her closet.

Sophie flicked through Eve's nicest clothes, piece by piece. "Some of these just scream *Anne of Green Gables*."

"You like that book? It used to be my favorite!" Eve heard her voice go up an octave like it did when she got overly excited. She coughed as if to cover up what they'd both heard.

"Not really, no." Sophie's tone reminded Eve that Sophie hated her.

Sophie laid out a few items on Eve's bed and placed them

together in different combinations. Her focus reminded Eve of an artist before her canvas. She explained to Eve which pieces worked with which and why, both because of the colors and because of how they flattered one body part or another.

"This one's for Monday." Sophie pointed to a skirt and dressy shirt. "And this one's Tuesday . . ." And she went through the whole week as if she were setting up a clothing syllabus.

Eve couldn't hide her skepticism. "Um . . . Those are a little . . . fancy? For school? A little showy?"

"Showing what?" Sophie snapped. "Your chest you're incredibly lucky to have? Your really nice clothes?" She shook her head. "Just be happy about it."

Eve shook her head, too. "You don't understand."

"What's that supposed to mean?" Sophie stood by the bed, hand back on hip. "Cuz I'm flat?"

"No! I just mean you don't get it. What it's like to be stared at like that." Eve remembered the stares, oh gosh, those stares, which she'd gotten all summer at the pool, while she was just trying to have fun and go down the slide with Nessa like they always had.

Sophie let out an angry laugh. "You think I don't know what it's like to be stared at? Are you kidding me?"

"I—I—that's not . . . that's not what I meant . . ." Eve fumbled for what to say.

"You know, there've been other lists before. There have been lists written on bathroom walls. There have been surveys of which girls have the best smiles, clothes, stuff like that. I've always won those. I've been stared at plenty. The difference is that I embrace it."

"Well"—Eve tried to be brave and push back on Sophie Kane—"I *don't*. And those are special-occasion clothes, anyway. They're too formfitting to wear to school," Eve said. "Ever since . . ." Last summer when her body had changed its size.

"They're not!" Sophie spat back.

Eve almost said "They are!" but she didn't want to turn this into a pointless fight. Eve tried to remember that if she did what Sophie said, if she could keep Brody's interest and get his trust, then she could go back to T-shirts. "I just don't want to dress, like, *for* other people, you know?"

"You know what?" Sophie picked up one of the shirts on Eve's bed, went toward the mirror, and held it up in front of herself. "Whether it's to try to look like number one or not, it's okay to just wear something that makes you feel good, you know? Like, I would feel good wearing this. Even if I wasn't trying to *be* anything." She spun around to Eve and posed. She went to grab some of the other shirts and repeated the same routine.

"But . . ." Eve felt herself genuinely wanting to know what Sophie thought. "What if my brother's shirts *do* make me feel good? And it feels good to not be stared at?"

"Aren't you kind of wearing them for 'other people' then, too?" Sophie put one of Eve's skirts in front of her waist and swayed side to side a little. "You're not wearing them because they make *you* feel good. You're wearing them because of how you want *other* people to see you. Or *not* see you. Right? Same thing, kind of. Here, put this on." Sophie tossed her a different skirt and a necklace she'd found in the jewelry box. "See if you feel good."

"Okay," Eve relented. "I'll put it on."

Eve went into her closet and changed. Did she wear the big shirts only because of other people's opinions? She wasn't sure.

When she came out, Sophie said, "Feels nice, right?" and went toward the closet to hang up all the outfits she'd created.

It felt okay. Yeah.

"Your wardrobe for the week," Sophie declared. Then she went back to the makeup and motioned for Eve to sit down on the edge of the bed. Sophie pulled a chair in front of her to begin their makeup tutorial.

"So what did Brody say when you said yes to going to the Halloween dance with him?" Sophie asked as she picked up some sponges and concealer.

"I'm not putting that on my face!" The sponges looked like sea creatures.

"You're right." Sophie sifted through more items. "This foundation is too dark for you. You have, like, no tan at all. Have you ever seen the sunlight?" She tsk-tsked Eve. "Forget it. We'll just start with a little concealer under the eyes and then try out eye shadow colors. Your eyes are stunning."

"Oh." Eve blushed for real this time. "Thanks."

"And these colors will really bring that out, so don't forget that this is your palette," she explained like a strict teacher.

As Sophie played around with little circles of eye shadow colors on the top of Eve's hand, testing out shades of blue and violet against her skin, she asked again, "So what'd Brody say when you said yes to the dance?"

"Oh, I never actually said yes. I avoided him the rest of the week, to be honest. I didn't know what to say."

Sophie smacked a hand against her knee. "*What?*"

"I—" Eve couldn't finish before Sophie cut her off.

"Give me your phone." Sophie held her hand out.

"Um. No."

"What? Give me your phone!" She emphasized each word with more and more annoyance.

"I can't!"

"Where is it?" Sophie searched Eve's room. She checked low to the ground, looking for outlets.

"Don't!"

"Eve Hoffman. If you wait and wait to do something because you're scared, then nothing ever gets done. Where is it?"

"No, it's not that! It's Shabbat, I can't use it!" Eve sighed.

"So . . . what's that mean?" Sophie asked.

Should she try to explain it? "Well, there are all these religious laws that on Shabbat you can't do stuff like tear toilet paper or turn on the lights." Oh man, now Sophie would definitely judge her. "But my family doesn't follow all that."

She was confusing Sophie. She'd try again. "When my brother Abe and I had our bar and bat mitzvahs, um, these big parties we have, my parents wanted us to pick one action for Shabbat that honors the deeper meaning of the day. And I felt like the meaning of the day is to quiet your mind. Rest. So on Saturdays, Shabbat, my brother doesn't use the internet and I stopped using my phone." She paused. "Well, I'm trying to stop."

"Huh." Sophie appeared to be processing all of it. "'Quiet your mind.' Doesn't sound so bad."

Eve thought she'd caught Sophie in an argument she couldn't win—religious protest. Yet Sophie's palm stayed out, waiting.

"Still," Sophie challenged, raising her eyebrows, "how badly do you want to go back to nobody noticing you in your baggy shirts, huh?"

Eve sighed and nodded toward the door. "In the kitchen. By the microwave."

Sophie retrieved the phone, put Eve's surrendering thumb on it to get past the password, and spoke out loud as she wrote. "Brody, sorry I didn't write back yet. TBH this is my first date. Smiley-blushy face. I'd love to go to the Halloween dance with you. What are you going as?" She dropped the phone down on the bed. "Done."

Guilt rose up in Eve as she raced to her phone and shut it off again.

"Back to the eyes?" Sophie picked up an applicator.

Eve returned to her spot on the bed and obediently closed her eyes, but she couldn't help herself from saying, "I hate this."

"The violet is the winner." Sophie ignored her, and went on to explain which eye colors worked best with which shades.

"Okay." The thought of what Brody might write back filled Eve with anxiety. She could hardly take in the detailed information on colors and ways of patting and spreading paints on her face. But she tried.

As Sophie plugged in a hair straightener under Eve's desk, she said to her, "Look. I actually believe that you don't want to be number one. At first I wasn't sure, but, hey, look at you. Pretty obvious. And I'm with you—I don't think you're the most beautiful girl in the world, either. I mean, you're fine. There's just no such thing. You were chosen as the prettiest by one person, but then everyone else just took that as 'the truth,' and now everyone believes it. It's not *real*. Sure, you're, like, really pretty. But if someone woke up tomorrow and put Rose Reed as the new number one, everyone would want to look like her instead." Sophie visibly shuddered.

"What are you going to do to my hair?" is all Eve could manage to say.

"I'm going to take the Shirley Temple out of it," Sophie answered.

As a silence passed between them, they heard their sisters laughing down the hall.

"Things were a lot easier back then, huh?" Sophie's voice softened.

"Yeah."

"Ya know, it's funny . . ." Sophie's eyes stayed on the straightener as its light turned to red and it began to steam a little. "You have this wild curly hair, and to look prettier, you have to straighten it. I have straight hair, and to look pretty I curl it." Sophie let out a funny little laugh. "Opposites."

"You don't *have* to," Eve offered.

Sophie turned to her, sharp. "You have no idea what I have to do."

19

SOPHIE

"Not everybody has it as easy as you, okay?" Sophie couldn't stop herself. This girl knew *nothing*. "Some of us have to work a little harder, let's just say that."

"You're so pretty, though. You don't *have* to work hard." Eve kept turning her head to respond to Sophie, and Sophie kept shifting it back to the right angle in order to straighten her hair.

"Ha. Pretty is different than pretti*est*, I guess," Sophie groused. She immediately regretted saying it. It made her sound jealous. "But whatever," she added.

"So you do all this every morning?" Eve turned her head back to Sophie. "*Really*?"

"Of course!" Sophie adjusted Eve's head again, a little more forcefully this time.

"Why would you even want to?" Eve went on. She was getting chatty. "Didn't you say that what people think of as pretty could change really easily? Like if the list changed, everyone's opinions would change? So just decide what's prettiest to *you* and do that!"

"*I'm not the one who gets to decide*! Don't you get it?" Sophie felt her voice begin to crack, and she stuffed her anger in deep.

The word "pretty" was starting to swirl around in her head until it didn't mean anything anymore.

Eve's curls steamed.

"That's confusing." Eve wouldn't let up.

Little Eve Hoffman wasn't so quiet all of a sudden. Maybe this was what happened when you had the bad luck of having to get to know her in her big, fancy house. It's also what happened whenever you did anyone's hair. Sophie had heard lots of secrets from people in her building when she cut their hair for them.

"Ya know what?" Sophie felt a wisp of the anger slip out. "You're judging me for the way I look, okay? You're judging me for liking to look a certain way. So maybe you're not the saint you think you are."

"Oh my gosh!" Eve turned around all the way to face her, nearly burning a cheek in the process. "No, I wouldn't judge you! I'm not!"

But Sophie put an end to it. "Let's turn on some music." She picked up her phone and put it on shuffle. Some country music came on.

They didn't speak again for the amount of time it took a country singer to tell the story of how he got his favorite truck.

"Do you know who Emily Dickinson is?" Eve finally asked her, breaking through the sound of the twangs.

"Um, no." Sophie watched the ends of Eve's oak brown curls turn into streams of flattened strands.

"She's who I'm doing the biography assignment on. What about you?"

Eve was trying to be nice now. Fine. "Audrey Hepburn," Sophie told her.

"Oh, cool! Well, Emily Dickinson was a famous American poet. Like, the most famous."

"Gotcha."

Eve probably assumed Sophie didn't read. Not true. Sophie read every school assignment. She got As on every paper. Eve probably thought Sophie was stupid just because she wore makeup. She probably didn't even know that in addition to being a famous actress, Audrey Hepburn also spent most of her life helping people all around the world. Both things were awesome.

"She inspired me to write poems, actually, even though mine are pretty bad," Eve went on. Maybe getting your hair done was like the confessionals at the church where her dad used to take her sometimes. When you couldn't see someone's face, it made it easier to tell the truth. "Anyway, I learned that Emily Dickinson never went outside! Like . . . ever. She just read and wrote poetry and letters in her room, all the time. Does part of that sound great to you? I think it sounds amazing."

Sophie could see from Eve's neck that she was blushing. Eve really was a Disney princess, Sophie thought. She probably sang to birds.

"She didn't want to have to go outside and deal with the world, I guess," Eve went on. "And I just don't quite fit in in the hallways with a hundred people, you know?"

"This Emily Dickins sounds just sad to me. And loaded. Staying in your room all day writing 'roses are red' or whatever? Ignoring the world?" *And it must be nice not to need to go out and make an actual living*, Sophie didn't say out loud.

"No, it wasn't like that!" Eve insisted, shaking her head.

The more she talked, the less Eve sounded like the quiet girl from school. Sophie found *this* Eve much more interesting.

"Stop moving your head!" Sophie commanded. "And don't forget that when you're doing this, you need to start from the scalp and slowly pull the straightener down to the tips, okay? Actually, try it yourself real quick." Sophie handed Eve the straightener and smirked as Eve struggled. "Anyway, I'm just saying, it's okay to be romantic and stuff, but it's not always the real world. Maybe Emily Dickins could have used some time in the hallways."

Eve said nothing except "Dickin*son*" and handed the straightener back to Sophie.

"Is that her?" Sophie nodded to a book on Eve's bed stand with Emily's name and a picture of her, she assumed. "I wonder what number she would've been on the list," Sophie said, and, to her surprise, Eve chuckled.

"That's pretty funny!"

"She's kinda cute, really." Sophie found herself giggling, too.

Sophie heard her phone ding. She went to check it. "It's the Choir Room Trio text."

"Yeah? What's it say?" Eve asked.

"I thought you weren't allowed to use your phone," Sophie teased.

"You can tell me what's on *your* phone!"

"Nessa says that Brody, Caleb, Winston, Aidan, and Tariq

are posting a bunch of nasty comments under girls' pictures about what number they are on the list."

"Disgusting."

"Typical."

The phone dinged once more.

"What else?" Eve asked.

"Oh, Nessa asks how the makeover is going."

"Well?" Eve asked. "How is it going?"

"Finished," Sophie answered.

She stood in front of Eve and took in the full view. Wow. Sophie had turned this girl into a movie star. She led Eve to the full-length mirror on the back of Eve's bedroom door.

"Voilà." Sophie couldn't help herself—she smiled, thin lip and all.

Eve gasped. "I look—I—I look—"

"Like a goddess," Sophie said. She curtsied in her jeans.

Eve spun in a circle, even though her skirt didn't twirl at all.

"See? Kind of fun, right?" Sophie went to Eve and adjusted her skirt a bit.

Then, still staring at herself, Eve awkwardly moved her shoulders in a little shimmy.

Sophie laughed. "Glad you like it."

"Oh my—" Eve said.

"For a famous poet wannabe, you're pretty bad at saying words," Sophie said, still laughing.

Eve turned to her and declared, "I love the eye part!"

"It's called eye shadow."

Eve flipped back to the mirror and kept moving her shoulders, but then her fingers started snapping and her whole body joined in. "And I love this song! Who is it?" she asked, dancing without any of the grace of a Snow White. More like one of the Disney sidekick characters. It was kind of funny.

Sophie knew this song too well. "My dad's band," she said, dismissing it and grabbing her phone to change it. How embarrassing.

"I love it!" Eve repeated.

Sophie changed it to a Top 40 playlist. "Don't."

"But it's so—"

"He's a jerk," Sophie cut Eve off.

Sophie kind of couldn't believe she was saying this to Eve Hoffman. She didn't talk about her dad. Ever. But there they were, doing that.

Eve didn't speak for a second, and she stopped dancing. Then she looked back into the mirror as she said to Sophie, "Nessa and I call jerks 'Malfoys.' And if they're really bad, then 'Voldemorts.'"

"Sooo nerdy." Sophie cringed, but laughed. She turned up

the new song as if to drown out the sound of her dad and erase it from the room.

The door burst open, and their little sisters danced their way inside, both dressed up in Eve's mom's clothes.

"I THINK HANNAH IS MY BEST FRIEND!" Bella yelled to Eve as the music pounded.

Sophie gave in and danced, too. She grabbed her little sister's hands, and they spun around together. Eve continued her goofy moves, her fingers snapping and her knees wobbling side to side. Maybe this was the Eve Hoffman that Nessa got to see.

As the song ended, they turned to the door and saw Eve's mom standing in its frame, a bemused look on her face.

"How's that school project going?" she asked, but not in a stressed-out way. More like she actually knew they weren't doing one and didn't care.

But when she took in Eve's face and hair, her smile disappeared.

"Oh, honey," she said as Sophie went over to her phone to turn off the music. "You look . . . so different."

Sophie knew in that moment that Eve's mom was judging her. She probably thought Sophie was a "bad influence." Maybe Eve's mom could tell that Sophie's clothes looked fancy, but were really used. Some of them homemade, sewed on her grandma's old sewing machine. Her mom had taught her how. Maybe Eve's mom saw the smudges all over Sophie's makeup bag, sitting next to Eve's chair, and wondered why her stuff was so dirty. Maybe she'd even figured out that Sophie wasn't from their neighborhood. Did parents know about other kids' parents in town? Maybe Eve's mom knew that the Kanes lived in Silver Ledge Apartments, or that her mom served people at a diner on the side of Greer Road. And even though there was nothing wrong with that, a lawyer or a doctor or something, which Eve's parents totally must have been, might think there was.

"We should go," Sophie said to the rich girls and their mom as she grabbed her stuff and threw it into her backpack. Bella came to her side.

"Oh." Eve's mom sounded surprised.

"Oh," Eve parroted in the same way.

"You need a ride home, honey?" Eve's mom asked.

"No, it's so close," Sophie answered, and she headed off from the huge, happy Hoffman home with Bella, still bopping around and singing, unaware that she would never be in the same world as someone like Hannah Hoffman.

She would have to make her own world.

20

EVE

After the Kanes left, Eve sat in front of her mirror. Oh my goodness. She looked like one of the portraits at the Detroit museum. And without her curls she seemed . . . older.

But could she do this on her own on Monday? Sophie had left a list of instructions, but could Eve really manage the right mix of lip and eye shadow colors and the knot-free hair? The one time she'd tried to straighten it on her own, it had frizzed out in all directions like she'd been struck by lightning. Nessa had taken about a thousand pictures.

As the sun set, and havdalah ended, Eve turned on her phone.

Texts lit up one after the other like stars appearing in the night sky, almost all of them from Brody Dixon.

oh man I cant tell you how glad I am youll go w me

not sure about my costume yet lol whats yours

i bet youre gonna look so beauitufl at the dance

we should hang out next week id love to get to know u better

u around? I have rehearsals. Maybe before or after?

u there

She almost texted the Choir Room Trio, *I can't do this*, but she stopped herself. She stood in front of the mirror once again.

Maybe the list was right. Maybe she was *really*, *uniquely* pretty. She *did* have a mouth that naturally pouted, just like her mom. And Sophie had told Eve that her eyes were "stunning." Inspecting her reflection, she saw it was true. They were so brown and dark that, looking into them, it felt like they never ended, like the swirls of soil brown went all the way to the middle of the earth. In the mirror she could see how the violet color shading them gave the brown of her irises a new glow, a hum, just like Sophie had said it would.

She felt guilty as she thought it, but still, she thought that maybe, just maybe, she *was* the prettiest.

Sophie sure knew how to give a makeover.

Eve texted Brody back.

Sorry! Just getting these now. Busy day.

Oh no, why did she have to use an exclamation mark? And she couldn't explain Shabbat to him, could she?

I was gonna be Juliet. Haha. I have this old Renaissance dress from the Renaissance Faire. But you be whatever!! I can meet you after rehearsal on Monday, if you want. I was going to wait for Nessa, anyway. So I'll see you then?

That was a lie. She had never planned on seeing Nessa rehearse.

That night she was pretty, and made up, and a liar.

Sophie's words repeated themselves in her mind: *You're judging me for liking to look a certain way.*

Was she? She didn't know. She didn't know if she was supposed to not like this face in the mirror, or only like it bare, or not think of it at all.

The face in the mirror didn't make sense anymore.

21

THE CHOIR ROOM TRIO

NESSA: **ok so the first real rehearsal tomorrow is the moment of truth**

EVE: **Why?**

SOPHIE: **because that's when you have to get brody to fall in love with you/trust you/etc**

NESSA: **what she said. stay late. go to the library or whatever. tell him youll meet him. my mom or dad can drive us home after.**

SOPHIE: **then you'll start sitting with me at lunch. sorry, nessa.**

NESSA: **i cant come? [GIF of Rachel from *Friends* going "Aw pretty please?"]**

SOPHIE: **that just gets too complicated**

NESSA: **i was kidding genius. ill pass thanks. plus the cast has been sitting together a lot and i prefer my theater friends to Fake Eve—no offense eve. did you notice that literally zero theater girls got in the top 50? maybe we need to change our search to someone who really hates musicals. also, isnt that a form of prejudice?**

SOPHIE: **moving on nessa do your best to find out his passcode to his phone**

NESSA: **on it. we need a tech genius on this. eve could your bro help**

EVE: **If Abe knew who wrote the list he would actually punch him.**

NESSA: **and . . . the problem is . . . ???**

EVE: **oh come on**

SOPHIE: **ok goodnight**

NESSA: **remind me what your job is again**

SOPHIE: **my job is managerial**

NESSA: **omg goodnight**

EVE: **see you tomorrow**

SOPHIE: **light eye shadow. straightened hair! the shirt with those sleeves!**

NESSA: **oh boy this is gonna be a disaster**

22

NESSA

Eve came into rehearsal that Monday afternoon right as the musical director told the ensemble to leave and asked the two leads to stay to begin work on their songs. Eve, newly dolled up, sat quietly in the theater's back row. She gave Nessa a little wave.

"It's never too early to dive in!" Mr. Rhodes chirped, turning his sheet music to the show's big ballad, and Nessa loved him so much in that moment.

As she and Brody began to sing, Nessa spotted Eve look up from the pages of her notebook and gaze at him. Gross.

Brody made the love in the song feel real, even if he sang like a toddler who had just jumped into ice-cold water.

But didn't Eve know that he was a bad guy in real life? He wrote the list! How could she like him? Who was this girl who didn't tell Nessa about boys asking her to dances? This girl getting crushes on monsters?

She felt the urge to mess with the harmony a little so Brody would make a mistake and maybe freak out at her and yell or something, so that Eve would remember he was mean.

Nessa believed Eve when she insisted that all the attention from the kids in school bothered her. But that day, coming to school with the "new look," Eve hadn't exactly seemed devastated. She even swished her straight hair behind her shoulder a couple of times in a move Nessa could only describe as Sophie-rific.

Nessa missed Eve's curls.

Right as rehearsal ended, Nessa pulled out her phone and texted Sophie: **brodys voice sounds like the sound cats make before they vomit, but guess who seems to like it, anyway?**

To which Sophie responded **ew. And more ew.**

Sophie may have been incredibly stuck-up, but at least she saw Brody for what he was.

As Nessa headed out of the auditorium she mouthed to Eve, "Record it!" Eve was supposed to try to get him to confess. Somehow.

Eve's befuddled face confirmed that she didn't know how to lip-read. This was hopeless. Did Nessa always have to be the one in their friendship who knew how to get things done?

And if Sophie's plan did work, and Eve did get Brody to admit to writing the list, if she didn't record it for proof, who would believe Eve Hoffman over Brody Dixon?

No one.

Nessa was on it, though. She'd keep pretending to ignore him, but she'd watch his every move. She'd find a clue, a hint, a *something*.

As she waited for Eve to mess it all up, Nessa headed to the bathroom next to the auditorium.

Inside stood Lara Alexander, dabbing under her eyes with crumpled toilet paper.

"Oh, hey." Lara tossed the toilet paper into the trash and faced the mirror to reapply some eyeliner.

"Hey." Nessa stood by her and pretended to fix her hair in the mirror, even though it already looked good. "You were awesome at the read-through the other day."

Lara gave her a closed-mouth smile. "Thanks."

So what was Lara upset about? Still this stupid list thing? Nessa wasn't on it, either, and it didn't ruin *her* life. Couldn't Lara talk to the counselors?

"You really are better than me." Lara nodded vehemently as she sniffled.

"No, no, I'm not!" Nessa *was* better overall. But Lara was still great!

"You are. And that's okay." Lara pulled out some mascara. "It's okay," Lara repeated as if to convince herself. "Ya know, it's just . . ." Lara took a breath and strengthened her voice. "I think I'm probably going to switch schools."

"Oh. Wow." So the rumors were true. This could really hurt the production. They needed her! "Before the show or . . . ?" Nessa tried to sound casual.

"I can't be here anymore!" Lara spat out. "People are laughing at me, like they think I think I'm pretty, they think I'm full of myself, and they're just so happy to see that no one would choose me for the top fifty prettiest. Well, they'd be happy to know I've *never* thought I was pretty and I've *never* liked how I looked. So they don't have to feel like it 'brought me down a peg' or whatever."

"I don't think people feel—" Nessa tried to say what she knew she should say, but Lara cut her off.

"Because guess what?" Lara turned to face Nessa. "I hate

everything about my face. Except my eyes. I like those. I used to wonder if I could be an eye model, like in ads where only eyes are seen. Like for mascara. Models start really young, like sixteen. My sister might end up modeling. She's almost sixteen, you know. And she's perfect. I've always hoped one day I'll look like her. But I look like *me*." Lara's voice cracked. She went into a stall to grab another chunk of toilet paper. "I'm so ugly."

"You're so, so beautiful," Nessa told her. And it was true. It was why Nessa had worried that Lara might get the part of Marian. It was also why, Nessa realized, she'd always assumed that Lara thought she was better than her.

Lara ignored her. "I just don't understand what happened to make everybody not like me. I used to think that when boys were looking at me it was because they liked me, but now I know it's because I'm a joke." Lara hid her face inside the tissue, and Nessa saw a droplet of an inky mascara tear hit the bathroom floor.

A flush came from one of the stalls. "Yeah, it's not so great," they heard someone say. A few moments later, Erin O'Brien came out. She handed Lara some more tissue paper and washed her hands. "But some of us never expected to be in the top fifty, fair or not. Some of us don't have famous parents and models for sisters."

"No! I didn't mean to complain, I—"

Erin left the bathroom without responding.

Lara looked toward Nessa for backup, and she seemed to take in Nessa for the first time. Maybe she thought about how Nessa wasn't on the list, either. "I'm not trying to say I have it worse than anyone or anything. But I can't help who my parents are! God!" She let out a sob.

"Look." Nessa held her shoulders. "Nothing is wrong with you or me or Erin. What's wrong is that stupid list. Like my mom says—it's cruel."

She grabbed some paper towel and helped Lara fix her makeup.

"Yeah," Lara said, though she didn't seem like she believed it. "Do you really think Hayley Salem is prettier than me?" she asked.

Nessa decided to stay with Lara for a little bit. Maybe Nessa owed it to her, for always having assumed Lara *was* full of herself, just like Lara had said.

Apparently, she could have benefited from being a bit *more* full of herself. They all could have.

23

EVE

Brody Dixon sat with her on a bench outside the front of the school.

As they spoke, Eve could see their breath, billowing out in white clouds.

"How'd you think we sounded?" he asked her.

"So good!" Eve heard her voice become airy and high-pitched.

Nessa had sounded perfect. Brody hadn't been great, but something about the way he performed the song . . . well, it made her *feel* what the song was trying to say. If that made any sense.

"It's sort of my biggest secret that I want to be an actor. I mean, everybody probably thinks I want to do sports, right? I mean, I'll do that, too. But I love movies. I want to be like that guy Hugh Jackman, you know? He plays Wolverine? He does action movies and stuff, but he also does really intense movies. I like that intense stuff. He even does musicals. I saw those movies, and that's why I tried out for the show. Oh, for my biography this year I'm doing Humphrey Bogart. You know that guy?"

Eve shook her head. "No. Sorry."

"Ah, it's okay. He did black-and-white movies and stuff."

"Oh, cool! Sophie is doing an old actor, too. Audrey Hepburn?"

Brody paused. "So you're friends with Soph now?"

Eve hesitated, and began to say, "Well, we've hung out . . . ," but Brody cut her off.

"Yikes," he mumbled. "Just don't take her too seriously, ya know? You think the show is looking good, though?" Brody asked again.

Eve nodded.

A huge grin lit up his face. And Eve couldn't help but think that Brody was extremely cute. His smile had this sly but sweet quality, like he knew something special about you that you didn't know about yourself.

She tried to remember that she was supposed to find evidence that he'd written the list. Nessa had practically screeched it at her as they'd left the theater. Sophie told her that in order to get evidence, she needed to make him vulnerable. But he already seemed pretty vulnerable. He just kept talking and talking.

"My dad—you'll see him when he picks me up—he's not so happy about the theater thing. It's so . . . what's the word? When something happens so much it's tired? Like when a guy in a movie races to get a girl at an airport before she flies away, or a bad guy gives away his entire plan at the end or something?"

"Oh yeah! Clichés! Oh, I hate them. They totally ruin even the best books!" As the words came out, she knew they were probably the wrong ones, but even if her hair and makeup were different, she was still Eve.

"Yeah, it's a cliché that my dad wants me to do sports and not plays. Like, Dad—be more original!" Brody smiled that smile again and said, "You're really easy to talk to. You know that?"

Eve pushed a strand of newly straight hair out of her eye with a gloved hand. "Nessa says that."

"Nessa's really cool, actually," he said.

Yeah. Eve knew that. Why "actually"?

"I'm gonna like acting with her," he added.

"She's the best," Eve said.

"Doesn't really fit the part, but she can do it great, anyway," he said.

Eve thought she knew what that meant, but she didn't know what to say. Should she respond, "She fits the part perfectly"? Should she explain to him that what he said wasn't kind?

"We have way too much homework, right?" Brody changed the subject again before she had the chance to say anything. He kept leading her in new directions in their conversation. How was she supposed to get any information out of him?

"Yeah," she said. And she thought of what Sophie might do. Sophie had all the confidence in the world. Eve pretended to be like Nessa, who was an actress, and then *act* like Sophie, who was . . . well, tough. "Ugh, it's hard concentrating on homework now, though," she said.

Brody raised an eyebrow.

"Now that I'm 'number one.'" She put on a forlorn face.

Brody just laughed. "Oh yeah, like it's so rough to be the prettiest girl in school."

Eve didn't know what to say. It *was* rough. It wasn't what he thought. But maybe he just thought it was a great thing, and that's why he'd written the list. To make her feel good. And then, the thought of him really liking her that much freaked her out.

"I guess," she said slowly, "someone put me there because they thought it was nice."

"Oh, hey, I see my dad." Brody jumped up and headed toward a sleek black SUV that swerved a few feet from where they were sitting. Eve watched as his dad gave him a thumbs-up and wondered if that was about her, or if that's just how they greeted each other. Weird.

As Brody and his dad drove away, Eve texted the Choir Room Trio, **He's not going to admit anything to me.**

You ready for me to call my mom for pickup? Nessa texted back right as she appeared beside Eve. "Hi." Nessa patted her back. "Bye!" She waved to Lara Alexander.

Nessa took a seat next to Eve on the bench.

"Ooh, Brody kept it warm for me."

"Yeah, call your mom," Eve said.

MAJOR FAIL Sophie wrote back to the group.

We will figure it out! We have until winter break for me to find his password or see something at rehearsals! Loads of time. As Nessa texted she said to Eve, "Sophie is really losing it, huh?"

No! you think we have that much time? by then, the

list will be set in stone. he will get away with it. dont you want it back to normal? eve, see you at lunch tomorrow. its your first day to sit with us. hell come in the middle after his guys are done eating.

ok ok, Nessa wrote back.

"Just be careful around him, okay?" Nessa bounced a little in the cold.

"What do you mean?"

"I mean, don't fall for whatever performance he gives you. He's not a good guy. Don't forget the things he's said before."

Eve didn't know if Brody was good or not, but she knew that he wasn't as bad as she'd thought before they spoke. And she also knew that all this phoniness exhausted her.

"Don't you look nice," Nessa's mom said to Eve as they hopped into the car.

Eve tied her hair into a messy ponytail. "Thanks."

"Come on, Brody is the worst, right?" Nessa turned toward Eve from the passenger's seat.

"He's . . . ," Eve began, trying to figure out what exactly he was.

"Oh no." Nessa raised her hands to her forehead and wailed, "You're falling for the whole handsome thing!"

"Nessa, stop the drama," Nessa's mom scolded as they

pulled out of the parking lot, the rainbow rosary clattering against the windshield.

"It's not the handsome thing! He's just not as bad as I thought he'd be!" Eve insisted.

"Oh no," Nessa repeated. "Handsomeness wins again." After a beat she added, "And so does cluelessness."

"What does that mean?" Eve asked her.

"Nothing."

They drove the rest of the way home in silence.

24

SOPHIE

For the next couple of weeks, as the dance approached, Eve sat with Sophie each day. Nessa sat with the *Music Man* kids, not-so-subtly watching Sophie's and Brody's tables.

Sophie gave Eve careful instructions on how to keep Brody's attention, and she wasn't doing as horribly as expected.

A few key rules for her time at the lunch table: No reading. No writing, either. No talking about Emily Dickinson or whoever. No mention of the Renaissance Faire. No staring off into space and daydreaming. Cut down on all the awkward pauses.

Who was this alien she'd suddenly become pretend friends with?

It turned out it was impossible to make Eve talk like a normal person. So Sophie spoke for her.

"So you like Brody, huh?" Rose Reed asked Eve one day.

Eve stammered some nonsense, and Sophie pronounced loudly, to the whole table, "I'm totally for it."

"What about Tariq?" Rose continued, looking past Sophie and right at Eve. "Or Aidan?"

Somehow Rose had inched her way closer and closer to Sophie, and she now sat next to Amina. A month ago she'd been on the ends of the tables. Rose being listed at number four still didn't compute. Why would Brody be *so* angry with Sophie that he'd do something like this?

"Aidan's always staring at you," Rose gossiped. "Like everybody, I guess!"

"Eve is going to the dance with Brody," Sophie told Rose.

Rose launched into a monologue about how she couldn't wait to go with Caleb as Princess Leia and Han Solo.

"She's a general now," Eve chimed in. "General Leia Organa."

An uncomfortable silence fell over the table.

"Yeah, for sure!" Rose chirped. "General!"

Sophie saw Liv and Hayley catch each other's eye and stifle a giggle.

At that point, the boys came to join them during their usual midlunch combination of tables. Brody scrunched himself between Sophie and Eve, talking to both of them about a bunch of stuff that Sophie blocked out. She couldn't take in one more Michigan football statistic or she'd pass out from boredom.

One good part about not being number one was that it was like a pressure valve had released a little bit. She didn't need to nod and smile as much. People were less interested in her reaction.

Maybe that's also why she'd stopped spending as much time on her hair, and started wearing her "weekend" eye shadow, the green color she liked a lot but knew didn't flatter her eyes as much as the bronze. No one seemed to notice, anyway. Plus, after what the Sophies had said about her in the hallway, she knew their real feelings about how she looked: *She knows how to 'look' pretty. Not* be *pretty. I mean, have you ever seen her without makeup?*

Sophie *liked* makeup, okay?

Anyway, she'd return to her full routine once Brody was caught and made irrelevant. For now, it wouldn't make a difference. Every day, slips of paper that read "#2" were sneaked into the slits in her locker.

Like she'd told Nessa and Eve in the choir room, popular kids were hated, not loved.

Over the past couple of weeks that Eve had begun to meld with the Sophies, Sophie observed that Eve's phone constantly buzzed. Eve would pick it up, glance at it, and put it down. Sophie would check hers, too, and see that it wasn't the choir room text. And she'd look over at Nessa and see her chatting away with the actor kids, so she knew the texts weren't from her.

That day, as Rose pestered Eve, Sophie saw a text show up on the main screen of Eve's phone.

As Sophie read it, she swallowed hard. Sophie had *never* been called that before.

When Rose was momentarily distracted by Hayley, Sophie spoke lowly to Eve. "I saw that text you just got. You have to show me the other ones."

Beneath the table, Eve handed her phone over with a reluctant sigh.

As Sophie scrolled through the texts, she struggled to hide her shock.

Eve's sloppily eye-shadowed lids closed for a moment. "Yeah," she whispered.

Text after text mentioned Eve's chest, or how she looked in whatever she was wearing that day, some in good ways and some in filthy ones. Some called Eve words that made Sophie shiver, thinking of stuff her dad had yelled at her mom during their worst fights.

"No one ever did that to me," Sophie whispered into Eve's ear. "Who's sending these to you?"

"I don't know whose numbers they are." Eve continued eating, head down, as if this as the last thing she wanted to talk about.

"I have almost everybody's numbers," Sophie answered, too loudly. "I can find out who these Malfoys are!"

Eve glanced at her, the corner of her mouth turning up slightly at "Malfoys." But then her face clouded over. "No, please don't. I don't want to know." Then she whispered almost inaudibly, "Just can't wait for this to end."

"What's wrong?" Rose Reed interrupted.

Sophie turned Eve's phone over and went back to her food. "Nothing. Just forget it. Anyway, moving on."

"Um . . . ," Rose answered. "I wasn't asking you."

The whole table turned to Rose. It was the first time in Ford Middle School history that anyone had rejected Sophie's directions.

Sophie dropped her fork onto her tray. "Excuse me?"

"I'm asking *Eve*," Rose went on. "What's your phone say, Eve?" She paused. "You don't have to check with Sophie to see if you can talk, okay?"

Sophie tried to remember what Rose's handwriting looked like. Had *she* been writing "#2" on those slips of paper? Had *she* put the Post-it on her back? Sophie looked to the other girls at the table, who had stopped eating, turning their foundation-heavy faces from Rose to Sophie and back again like they were watching a tennis match. Had one of *those* girls actually written the list? Were they all happy she was number two?

As Sophie prepared to respond, Eve jumped in.

"Oh, it was just a text about the dance. My costume," Eve said. "Amina, are you still going as Veronica?"

"Maybe," Amina said. "But I might want to be some kind of villain!"

In the movie version of their lives, Sophie thought, Eve might be trying to replace her. But in the real-life version, she knew, Eve was trying her best to get life back to normal. And also, in the face of the girls who were beginning to see Sophie as lesser than them, Eve might have been trying to protect her. Maybe.

"Hey." Sophie stopped Eve in the hallway after lunch

ended. "How long have you been getting those? Are the texts always that bad?"

"Since the list came out," Eve mumbled. "They just get worse. But I *really* don't want to talk about it, okay?"

"You need to tell someone!" Sophie insisted.

"And would that really make it stop?" Eve shook her head and hurried off.

If Sophie was honest with herself, she couldn't be sure it would.

PE had become unbearable. Twice a week, three classes all joined together on the field and battled it out.

When the sexes were split up, Sophie dominated, of course. She and Hayley were a regular Steph Curry and Kevin Durant. They slammed the volleyball into the grass during the spring and climbed the ropes on the indoor obstacle courses twice as fast as the other girls during winter. But when Ms. Meijer had the girls versus the boys, or mixed-sex teams, Sophie couldn't embarrass Brody or his guys by running too fast or playing unbeatable defense. So she just slowed down a little. She stayed farther back from the basket or the goalposts.

That day, Ms. Meijer chose boys versus girls for soccer.

Sophie eyed the boys gathered across from her, wondering which of them had written those texts to Eve. They must have thought they were pretty funny, huh? Using words they'd heard their favorite singers and rappers say. Not knowing or caring how it felt to be on the receiving end of those disgusting phrases.

She couldn't wait to score a goal.

As Ms. Meijer set up the orange cones, Brody hollered from across the patch of grass that separated his team and Sophie's. "Hey, Soph! How's it feel knowing you'll be number two *again* today?"

Sophie heard a laugh behind her and turned to see that it came from Rose, who quickly covered her mouth. Brody's friends gave high fives, and even the boys who would have *loved* to take her to the Halloween dance, boys she had never even spoken to, not out of meanness but more because she'd had no reason to, they laughed, too. It wasn't even a funny joke.

Sophie tore off her sweatshirt, knowing she'd be steaming hot once she kicked into a higher gear, and she didn't care where it landed.

The game began.

This time, Sophie didn't slow down.

She swooped in on the ball, shuffling it toward the goal and kicking it with all her might. Take *that*, Unknown Numbers. Take *that*, Brody.

Two minutes in and her team had scored the first point.

"Not even breaking a sweat out here," she announced loudly enough for everyone, especially Brody, to hear.

He bellowed something in response, but she was already moving, already hustling so hard that Ms. Meijer didn't even need to yell "Hustle!" the way she always had before when they'd competed against the guys.

Sophie grunted as she scored again.

Hayley came up to her, and they bumped chests like boys did and then laughed at how it hurt.

"Ouch! Let's not do that again!" Hayley cackled as Sophie practically galloped back to her spot on the field.

Sophie hadn't forgiven Hayley for what she'd said about her, but she'd team up with her against these kids any day.

As they all took a water break, Brody and Caleb practiced headbutting the ball. Ms. Meijer told them to quit it, and the teams faced off again.

"Looks like I'm not gonna be second place, after all," Sophie chirped in a sugary sweet voice to Brody.

"Yeah!" His eyes darted to the sides as if to check to see if everyone heard him. "But no guy wants to take Larry Bird to the Halloween dance, right?"

Caleb and Tariq snickered.

"Explains a lot," he said even louder.

"Hmmm." Sophie raised him a level in volume. Everyone was listening. "That's weird because it doesn't explain *why you tried to kiss me at your house last month.*"

Boom.

She heard a few "Awwww, mans!" and several kids in the crowd snickered.

Brody Dixon's face froze midjeer. His cocky mouth turned downward, and for a moment he looked like he had old man jowls.

Sophie couldn't stop herself.

She'd pretended for so long.

He'd been at the top, and she'd been at the top; how dare he try to bring her down? What made him deserve to stay there more than her?

Gets-everything-he-wants Brody Dixon couldn't handle a girl not wanting to kiss him? Please. And she was supposed to act like that was okay? She was supposed to act like any of this was okay? No.

She raised her volume once again. She wanted every single kid to hear.

"Poor Brody. It must be so sad for you that I *didn't kiss you back* and I'm beating you now *so hard*!"

Sophie heard the whistle blow, and she didn't look back at the damage she'd caused. Without one more glance toward Brody for the rest of the game, she took her team to victory.

25

THE CHOIR ROOM TRIO

NESSA: **Soph, what did you say to brody today???**

SOPHIE: **why**

EVE: **What??? Is that why he seemed all quiet?**

NESSA: **because every single human on earth is talking about it. he tried to kiss you?? you turned him down????**

SOPHIE: **whatever moving on did he text u tonight**

EVE: **He won't STOP texting me.**

SOPHIE: **good**

NESSA: **btw lara is pretty upset about the list. its sad. she really might transfer schools**

SOPHIE: **yeah like she has anything to complain about. shell transfer to Greenmount. shell go to a BETTER school!**

NESSA: **hey thats mean**

SOPHIE: **and you're never mean?**

you know what never mind

NESSA: **I don't know maybe she could help us. the more the better right?**

EVE: **what if she actually wrote the list though? What if we are wrong?**

SOPHIE: **why wouldnt she put herself on it then . . .**

EVE: **I don't know, maybe she WANTS to go to another school.**

SOPHIE: **EVE. BRODY WROTE THE LIST. TRUST ME. ACCEPT IT.**

NESSA: **yeah shes right. brody wrote it not lara alexander!!! ugh how can you be defending brody. gross**

SOPHIE: **yeah are you a double agent now or something**

look he will like another girl soon and it wont be you

EVE: **I'm not defending Brody!**

SOPHIE: **okay wow maybe you haven't gotten**

anything useful from him about the list because youve fallen for his nice guy act

but we need you to stick to the plan

the halloween dance is the perfect time to record him admitting it

he might not like you for much longer

and it wont be long before he kisses you trust me

EVE: What?!?!?!?!?!

NESSA: aw geez don't say that i just ate dinner ill get sick

EVE: But we hardly know each other!!!!!!

SOPHIE: did you really just say that

NESSA: evie look how stressed youre making sophie

EVE: I am not falling for his act!

SOPHIE: whatever you know what im going to bed goodbye

NESSA: sophie always leaves in a huff lol

EVE: haha

NESSA: she never leaves a room without being like [GIF of reality show actress storming off and kicking a table over, then throwing over a bookcase on the way out of the room]

EVE: hahahahaha omg Nessa

SOPHIE: **very funny**

NESSA: **youre the funny one**

SOPHIE: **okay Im serious now bye bye**

NESSA: **she's doing it again lolololol**

EVE: **hahaha**

SOPHIE: **SOME OF US HAVE HOMEWORK TO DO GOODNIGHT**

26

EVE

Text message, after homeroom, Curtis Milford:

you think you're so much better than me don't you

Text message, unknown number, during math class:

hey no 1. u always look so sad. smile. ☺

Text message, unknown number, end of math class:

is it tissue in there or padding

The day before the Halloween dance, an unfamiliar voice came from behind Eve's open locker door.

"How's it going?"

She shut her locker to find Winston Byrd standing there, his hands wrapped around his backpack straps, his shoulders hunched over a bit as if he wasn't yet used to being so tall. For an instant, she wondered whether he'd sent her any of the text messages, and which ones.

"It's okay." She felt her face flush as pink as cherry blossoms. *Why, God? Why did her blood vessels betray her like this?*

Winston looked like he was about to say something right as Brody came toward them from the boys' bathroom.

Two seventh graders waved at Brody. He threw them a slight nod of the head as he strutted by.

"Hey, Byrd!" Brody smacked Winston's back so loudly Eve heard a thump. "Hanging by my girl's locker, huh?" His teeth gleamed white under the harsh hallway light. "Joking, joking. What's up?" Brody propped an elbow against Eve's locker.

Winston seemed to force a smile. Eve hadn't known he wore braces. He never smiled with his teeth showing. "Nothing, nothing, man."

"You still coming with Caleb to my place before the dance?"

"Oh, um. Can't. But I'll see you there."

"Cool." Brody turned away as if dismissing him.

"All right, see you guys at lunch."

But Winston didn't sit with those guys at lunch anymore,

Eve realized. In fact, she hadn't seen him with that group of boys for a week or so. Where had he gone?

My girl, Brody had called her. He had been joking, right? What did it mean to be "his" girl?

She decided to ignore it.

She and Brody really only spoke in school once or twice a day, and whenever she brought up the list Brody changed the subject quickly. But he texted her constantly.

crazy my bday is on fri the 13th this yr. luv when that happens

my dads gf caroline picked the movie tonight and its actually pretty good wow didnt think she had it in her

yr bff Nessa wont stp askng me to run lines can u tell her to lay off a bit lolol

i mean caroline isnt so great but i can see why my dad is w her. shes like miss america level gorgeous. could never say that to my mom tho. ur parents still 2gther yea?

have you ever wondered what color the ocean would be if blue didnt exist. lol just thinking about stupid stuff sry

It was actually sort of sweet how he felt comfortable

enough to talk to her about his dad's girlfriend, and to share his most random thoughts.

As she walked into the cafeteria that day, a few teachers were hanging up pumpkin and skeleton decorations on the walls. Nessa blew her a kiss from the lunch line, and Eve took her prepacked meal out of her backpack and headed toward Sophie's table.

Earlier in the year, Eve's greatest distraction had been the desperate need to finish any final chapter of whatever book she had on hand. Recently, her distractions from schoolwork included whatever happened in the hallways and during lunchtime. She hadn't even finished the last book she'd started, she realized as she arrived at the Sophies' table.

But Sophie wasn't sitting there.

Rose Reed sat in Sophie's old spot.

Eve texted Sophie and asked where she was. Eve couldn't do lunch without her! Eve still felt like she wore a costume. Like she was a spy. However, even though she'd never admit it to anyone, she *did* like the way the new outfits fit on her. When she put them on in the morning she'd catch herself lingering in front of the mirror.

But then at school, when people's eyes fell on the wrong places, she wanted her old life back so fiercely she could scream.

Eve began to turn away from the table so that she could find Nessa and ask her where Sophie had gone. Before she could move, she felt a hand on her arm.

"Where you going?" Brody asked with a smile.

Eve stayed at the Sophie-less table. On her phone, a message from Sophie appeared:

I can't go back there today. Sorry, it said.

And Eve could see why. A whole day later, and everyone was still talking about the soccer game.

"Did you hear, Evie?" Rose asked her, and Eve cringed a little at hearing the name that only Nessa and her family used. "Sophie's so mad you're number one that she's making up stories that she turned Brody down. Pathetic!"

Hayley and Liv shook their heads along with some other girls at the table, but Amina said, "We don't know what really happened, guys."

Eve knew she should say something to stand up for Sophie, like Amina had. Eve knew that Sophie wasn't making anything up.

But it was easier to stay quiet until the subject changed.

All day long, Eve replayed Rose's comments in her mind and fretted about her own silence. Weren't those girls Sophie's friends? Why would they talk behind her back like that?

As school ended that day, she was so lost in her thoughts of Rose and Sophie that she hardly noticed Brody coming up behind her.

How did he always find her? She wondered if maybe he had memorized her class schedule. If so, he must *really* like her.

"Can you come over the day before the dance?" he asked her with a smile on his face. It always surprised her how kind his smile could be.

"I hope you're not listening to Sophie's stories about me," he added, speaking lowly. "She's crazy."

There it was. Another chance to speak up for Sophie, to defend her.

"Well . . . ," Eve began, but nothing else came out.

"So can you come by?" he asked again.

Eve thought of what Sophie had said. How he would try to kiss her soon.

"I have family stuff," she told him.

And Sophie's not crazy, she thought to herself as Brody waved goodbye.

27

NESSA

The night of the Halloween dance arrived. Nessa turned on her favorite mix of spooky choir music. When Sophie arrived at her house, Nessa jumped out with a monster mask on.

It didn't scare Sophie. But it was fun, anyway.

Eve was going to be late because she had to wait until after Shabbat dinner to meet them. Such a nuisance.

So there they were. She and Sophie Kane, alone. Sophie Kane, the girl who had had a million opportunities to speak to her throughout the years they'd gone to school together, but never had until she'd needed something.

Nessa's mom and dad welcomed Sophie in. Nessa's mom told them that they'd leave in an hour. Nessa checked Sophie's face for a response to her mom's Spanish, but she didn't catch one. Her mom had lived in the States since she was three and didn't even remember life in Santa Tecla, but some people in Glisgold treated her like she'd just arrived yesterday when they heard her speak in her native language.

When they got to Nessa's bedroom, Sophie shocked Nessa by not saying anything stupid like people usually did ("You speak Mexican?" or "I didn't know you were Mexican." *Oh my God, people. Read a book.*). Instead Sophie asked, "Do you speak Spanish, too? Is there any way you could help me with my Spanish homework? I'm bad. And I *can't* get a B. I just can't."

Nessa couldn't help but laugh. "Sure," she said.

"What's so funny?" Sophie asked.

Nessa understood almost everything in Spanish, but when she spoke it, people in her mom's family made fun of her accent. At least her dad spoke it as badly as her. Well, way, way painfully worse than her. That helped.

"I speak enough to help you out, let's just say that."

Sophie grinned and proceeded to take out an abundance of makeup tools.

"Thanks," Sophie said as she pulled out a powder brush.

Nessa couldn't shake the feeling that Sophie was using her again.

"Okay, let's get to work." Sophie was there to make Eve look Brody-confession-inducing amazing, but Nessa had insisted on help with her own costume, too. She wasn't convinced Sophie could pull it off, though.

Nessa showed Sophie a picture of the makeup look she wanted, and Sophie sighed.

"Not my usual specialty, but okay, I'll give it a shot," Sophie relented. "Professor McGonagall it is."

Sophie's costume appeared to be some kind of . . . pretty person? Cute girl? What was it exactly? Sophie and her friends dressed in these noncostume costumes every year.

"Okay, so spill it. What are you dressed as?" Nessa didn't bother hiding the disdain in her voice.

"I'm a dancer," Sophie answered as if it were obvious.

Nessa looked Sophie up and down. "Don't dancers wear leotards? Tutus or something?"

Sophie put her hands on her hips. "Wow, the costume police are really strict this year."

Nessa shrugged. "I'm just saying. Okay, let's do this."

After Sophie finished up and put the final bobby pin into Nessa's bun, she handed Nessa a hand mirror from the bed stand.

Nessa stared at her reflection. She looked incredible. "*Thank you*!" she said.

Sophie smiled approvingly. "Not bad," she admitted.

So Sophie got to be the most crushed-on girl in the eighth grade *and* she had serious makeup talent? What a nice life.

"Hey!" Nessa exclaimed, thinking of a way that Sophie could do something else for *her*. "You should do makeup for *The Music Man*! They make us do our own, but most people are really bad at it, and you'd make us all look so much better! We can trade homework help for *Music Man* makeup magic!"

Sophie grunted. "Yeah, right."

At that, the doorbell rang.

"Right on time!" Nessa yelled out.

Eve walked in, dressed in the Juliet costume she'd worn two years in a row.

Sophie looked Eve up and down and, without even saying hello, held up a makeup brush and declared, "You have to look *perfect* tonight."

As soon as they walked into the gymnasium, Sophie went off to the middle of the room to join her crowd.

"Okay, bye," Nessa said.

"Do you see him?" Eve asked her, fidgeting all about.

"Not yet." Nessa took her hand.

Eve squeezed Nessa's hand and went off to look for Brody.

Would Eve just slow dance with Brody or something and forget their whole plan? Nessa tried to have faith that her friend hadn't changed *that* much. Hey, at least her goofy Renaissance Faire costume, despite its newly snug fit, *screamed*, "I'm still the old Eve."

Nessa scanned the room for any other fun people. Lara Alexander, Erin O'Brien, and a couple of other kids from the show danced in their own little corner. Lara wore a gown and a crown and looked like actual royalty. Erin O'Brien had a red cardboard airplane around her chair and was dressed as Amelia Earhart. Nessa wove through some skeletons, zombies, and various types of princesses and superheroes as she headed toward that safe zone.

"Hey, is Brody here yet?" Nessa asked the crowd.

Erin rolled her eyes. "No, I don't think so. I would've smelled the cologne and ego."

Nessa snorted. "True."

A paper jack-o'-lantern hanging from the ceiling fell, and a couple of teachers scrambled to get its string out of a girl's hair. Amina, dressed as Catwoman, twirled around the dance floor with Hayley, who wore a costume as vague as Sophie's. Winston Byrd, that night the Green Hornet, and Caleb Rhines, Han Solo, stood in a corner under an art-class-made papier-mâché monster, arguing. Probably about sports. Caleb pointed a menacing finger at Winston's chest and shouted something. Okay, maybe *not* sports. Rose Reed, dressed as Princess Leia, came over and took Caleb's arm to lead him to dance.

But no Brody. And where had Eve gone?

Everyone looked different this year. Glam-ier. A bunch of the girls wore more makeup than she'd ever seen on them. This was probably the one night their parents allowed them to do that. But Nessa suspected that wasn't the only reason. Every girl's outfit screamed "*Put me on the list*!"

Whatever happened to simply wanting to win the costume contest?

But wait. Sophie was right; Nessa shouldn't act like the costume police.

She heard a group of voices over the music. They came from somewhere far off. The dancing stopped, and people began to crowd around something. A fistfight?

Wait, could it be Eve? *Was Eve okay*? Nessa felt her best-friend instinct kick into high gear, and she tried to run toward the action, but the crowd blocked her. She attempted to push her way through, but Nessa still couldn't see who was yelling or why. She saw Mr. Flynn coming from another side, also trying to get to the center of the noise, as another teacher rushed out of the room.

And then, nudging through the gawking bystanders, she saw what all the commotion was about. Standing right in front of Sophie and Eve, his hand on his hip as he tossed back the hair of his cheap blond wig, stood Brody Dixon dressed in the most horrifying Halloween costume Nessa could imagine.

28

EVE

Makeup covered his face: bright pink lips, eye shadow up to his eyebrows, mascara lazily smudged all around his eyes, and buckets of blush. Up close, Eve could see permanent marker drawn all over the roots of the messy blond wig. His clothing was reminiscent of Sophie's—a red tank top, tight jeans—but he'd attached an enormous price tag to it that read **50¢**. Around his neck hung a small poster board with a hastily scribbled **#2** on it.

And he wouldn't stop talking, his voice nasal and falsetto.

"OMG, my dad hasn't paid child support in foreeever. But that's probably because he's, like, in jail or whatever."

Eve's stomach lurched. She thought she might throw up.

Instinctively, Eve moved toward Sophie as Sophie croaked: "*He is not! Stop it!*"

"Seriously, like totally, I'm, like, white trash, like yeah."

"*Why are you doing this?*"

"OMG, gotta go wash the fleas out of my clothes!"

Sophie leaned over, her hands on her knees, unable to catch her breath.

Eve reached for her and held her up. "It's okay, Sophie, it's okay."

Mr. Flynn came toward them, yelling, "Hey, Brody! Hey!" The music had abruptly stopped.

"What is wrong with you!?" Eve screeched at Brody.

Everything Nessa had said about him had been true. His kind smile had meant nothing. He was as bad as they all claimed. How could she have thought any different for even an instant?

At Eve's words, Brody stopped the performance. "Ha. What? It's a joke." He put out a hand to Eve, as if she'd ever come near him again.

Couldn't he see she was literally holding up Sophie? That his little act had forced Sophie to buckle over?

Brody wore a laugh on his face, like he thought everyone else would laugh, too. And most did. Out of the corner of her eye, in the haze of her disgust, Eve spotted some of Brody's guy friends chuckling into their palms.

"You're disgusting!" Eve spat out as Sophie held tightly on to her arm, trying to keep her balance.

"Of course he's disgusting. He's dressed up as Sophie!" she heard Caleb say behind her. "So sensitive, geez!"

"Shut up!" another guy yelled from somewhere.

"Come here," Brody insisted, putting a palm out to Eve once again.

"Don't touch me!" Eve held her hand tight against her body in a fist.

The other day, when he'd called Sophie crazy, it had been a sign of some awfulness inside him. She *knew* she should've said something to him. Maybe because she hadn't said anything, he'd thought it was okay to do what he had done. *Why hadn't she said something*?

"Hey!" Mr. Flynn hollered as he continued to make his way through the crowd.

Brody moved toward Eve and touched her fist, trying to pull it to him.

"I *said* don't touch me!"

Seemingly out of nowhere, Winston Byrd shot out of the crowd and pushed Brody with all his might. "She said don't touch her! Stop!"

Brody probably would've fallen to the floor, but his guys caught him.

Caleb Rhines ran toward Winston, all three of the boys ignoring Mr. Flynn's pleas to stop. "What is wrong with you, man?" Caleb shoved Winston, who backed away and bolted out of the gym.

Mr. Flynn finally arrived next to Brody. "Come on, Brody, let's get out of here."

"Yeah, get out of here!" Sophie hissed.

Brody paused, grinning at her, nudging off Mr. Flynn's attempts to pull him away. "It's just a joke, *Silver Ledge*."

For a moment, Sophie seemed to morph into an entirely different person. The whole bottom half of her face quivered. Her shoulders wilted. Her mouth clamped shut, and then it tightened.

"Yeah, we know where you live. People talk, you know. Nice try keeping it secret, though," he went on.

As quickly as Sophie's spine had slumped over, it straightened. She held her head high. The Sophie that Eve recognized came back.

"Brody Dixon. Stop talking right now."

For the first time, no murmurs or hollers could be heard in the gym. The only sound was Mr. Flynn directing another adult across the room to come help him.

Sophie's jaw clenched. "I mean it. Stop." Sophie took a step toward him, not a quiver left in her.

Eve remained where she was. How did Sophie speak back to him with such courage?

And did he say Silver Ledge? The apartment building? Eve had never been there, but she knew some kids in their district lived there. Who cared?

"Oh. What?" Brody goaded her. "You don't want everyone to know you live in Silver Ledge? Like, a block from the jail?" Brody turned to the crowd and added, "I like my girls thrift store– and food stamps–free, you know?"

Some in the crowd gasped.

Eve tried to remember what had seemed sweet about Brody. Had it just been that he'd spoken to her? Told her about his dad's girlfriend? Shared with her that he wanted to be an actor one day, but his dad didn't like that? Was it just . . . his *attention* that she liked? How pathetic was Eve to let all that trick her? Attention had always been something she thought she hadn't wanted, and yet she'd fallen for it.

Sophie pointed a finger at Brody's chest. "People only like you because you're rich. You're a creepy, mean, disgusting excuse for a human being who will peak in high school before the world figures out you have no talent except for having a room for your ugly dog!"

Brody and his boys laughed. "What is she even talking about?" He turned to his friends. "Somebody's still mad I didn't ask her to the dance."

At this, Sophie stalked out of the room, her high heels like mallets on the drum of the floor.

Eve turned to follow, but at the sound of Brody's voice she stopped.

"Eve," Brody said in a command, hand out once more. "Come on."

"No." Eve could finally breathe as Nessa arrived by her side.

"What?" Brody's hand remained reaching toward her.

"Don't talk to me." Eve felt herself shudder. "Don't come near me, ever again."

The crowd behind her seemed to inhale as one, hushed.

Mr. Flynn at last succeeded in pulling Brody away. "Come on, now. Let's get out of here."

"Okay, fine!" Brody yelled back to the crowd as they left. "But, hey! Eve! Are you ever going to tell the truth?" He and Mr. Flynn neared the door. "Isn't is obvious?" he hollered to the entire eighth grade. "Eve Hoffman wrote the list herself! *She told me so*!"

At that, the kids behind Eve moved away from her, joining Caleb and the other guys. Eve felt them watching her, and knew everyone's feelings toward her had instantly flipped.

"It's true," Caleb told the crowd. "Eve wrote it. Brody liked her, so he didn't want to tell on her. But now . . ."

Could Eve turn to her classmates, explain to them that Brody and Caleb were lying? No one would believe Eve, no matter how awful Brody had been that night. All he had to do was say the word and Eve was done for.

She could stay, and try to fight back.

But something else mattered much more.

Eve grabbed Nessa's hand. They both knew what they had to do next.

Find Sophie.

29

SOPHIE

She sat on the piano bench with the lights off. Her secret was out. Her mascara streaked across her cheeks.

She'd thrown an insult at Brody that her mom had shouted at her dad one day. "You peaked in high school!" her mom had cried. He'd snapped back, "You too."

Knowing she'd repeated those words, even to Brody, made her ill.

When Nessa and Eve came into the room, Sophie couldn't lift her head to face them. Instead, she stared at the piano pedals. She worried that if she looked at their faces, she'd cry more.

"Brody's right, guys," she forced out. "I *was* mad that he didn't ask me."

She instinctively dabbed under her eyes with her shirt, and the sequins scratched her nose.

Crying was for the weak. But she felt weak.

"I wanted the most popular, richest guy in school to ask me to the dance," she continued with a sniffle. "I mean, everyone thought he would. Before this stupid list came out." Neither of the girls answered her, but she felt them move closer to the piano. "And he was right that I live in Silver Ledge, okay? But my dad isn't in jail!"

"Even if he was, that doesn't mean anything about you and shouldn't be an insult!" Nessa broke in.

Sophie held up a hand to stop Nessa from saying any more. "I didn't really care about 'justice,' okay? I wanted to find evidence so I could take down the list writer and get a new one written. Be number one, like I thought I was."

Sophie felt a sob lodge itself in her throat, but she gritted her teeth to hold it in. "I should've just let him kiss me! Then none of this would've happened!" The sob shot out of her. "I just . . . I don't know why, but I just didn't want to." Sophie put her head in her hands. She couldn't let Nessa and Eve see her like this. From far off, she heard the dance music start up again. "I just want to run away." Sophie heard her voice waver. "Get on a bus, take it to the train station, get on a train, take it across the country." She thought of her dad. How he had left. Where was he this month? Austin? She wiped her nose again. She had to keep it together. "But I can't. So I'll just run home." Sophie got up and headed toward the door, facing away from Nessa and Eve.

Nessa blocked her exit. "You think *I* cared about 'justice for all' or something?" Nessa confessed.

For the first time since Sophie had met her, Nessa appeared a little less confident.

Nessa took a breath. "Brody hurt my feelings that day. Before the assembly."

Sophie saw Eve snap her head toward Nessa. "*What*?"

Nessa nodded. "Yeah. He made it sound like Mr. Rhodes was doing me a favor for giving me the lead in the show. 'Cause I'm not a supermodel, I guess." Nessa didn't face Eve as she went on. "I'm just really tired of guys like Brody thinking they can be jerks like that and it's all good, you know?"

"It's not like I wanted to catch Brody for the good of everybody or anything!" Eve broke in loudly. "I was just thinking about myself! At first, I just wanted the attention to stop. I wanted to stop the stares. The endless stares. And then . . . I guess I liked some of Brody's attention, I think. But I should have known that something like this would happen . . . I'm so sorry. I can't believe what he did to you tonight, Sophie."

"Me either!" Nessa took Sophie's arm and led her back to the piano bench. Eve hurried along behind her.

"Okay, so *none* of us were thinking about how each other or other girls felt. Like I thought everyone was overreacting. And then the other day when I saw Lara Alexander *crying* . . ." Nessa sat down, and Sophie and Eve sat on either side of her. "I mean, how did I not think about how bad this felt for *everybody*? *Really* bad!"

"Wait, she was *crying*?" Sophie didn't know why, but that made her feel like crying again, too.

"Yeah! And Erin was just as upset, too . . . ," Nessa continued.

The three girls sat in silence.

"I don't think we'll ever get any evidence of who wrote it," Sophie said, finding herself wanting to break the quiet.

"Yeah, probably not," Nessa acknowledged.

"He's not going to admit it," Eve said with certainty. "He was never going to get close to me or anything, anyway. I don't think he's that kind of person," she added in a near whisper.

"Yeah," Sophie agreed. "He was always going to get away with it."

"And I mean, for all we know, he didn't even write it," Nessa offered.

"Time to give up," Sophie announced. "Brody wins."

"But he did write it," a voice said, drifting toward them from the back of the choir room. A boy's voice.

Eve let out a little yelp and hopped up from the bench.

"*For Pete's sake, what is it with people lurking in the back of choir rooms*?" Nessa hollered with a hand to her heart.

Sophie felt a fury rise in her. Who would listen in on her? How dare they?

"Show thyself!" Nessa marched over to the lights to turn them all on.

In the back of the room, Winston Byrd leaned his elbows over the back of a chair, hands clasped together.

"Hi, Phantom of the Opera," Nessa joked.

"Get out." Sophie stormed toward him. One of Brody's followers? How dare he invade *their* choir room?

"Wait! He defended Eve when she didn't want Brody to touch her!" Nessa giggled. "Pretty great!"

"Gross." Sophie shot her a glare. Sophie thought of her mom. Of Mrs. Jackson, who helped take care of Bella and had four grandchildren to take care of, too. Of all that Sophie had to do to get through these awful days. They didn't need help from any boy. "He needs to go." She arrived at his chair and motioned for him to leave.

"But what if he can help?" Eve suggested.

"We just decided this is all hopeless!" Sophie argued.

"Let's just hear him out." Nessa gestured for Winston to begin.

"Um . . ." Winston fumbled for words.

It took everything in Sophie not to snap, "Come *on*! Out with it!" but she knew Nessa and Eve wouldn't like that. She walked down with him to the first row choir seats, and all the girls sat as Winston stood in front of the piano and chalkboard and spoke.

"He brags about it all the time," Winston mumbled. "He talks about why he put each girl where. Why he left certain girls off."

Okay. Interesting. Why had he put her as number two? Was it just the kiss?

She shouldn't still care. She shouldn't! Why should she care what he thought after he ruined her life? But she did. She hated herself for it, but she did.

Before Sophie could ask about herself, Eve jumped in, her face all tortured and sad. "Why was I number one?"

"Maybe to cause drama?" Winston's low voice cracked a tiny bit. "He's such a jerk . . ."

It felt funny to hear one of Brody's guys saying that.

"And why would he tell people I wrote the list?" Eve asked.

"You embarrassed him," Winston answered.

And when Sophie heard that, she knew she didn't need to ask why she was number two. She'd been right all along. She'd turned him down and embarrassed him. That explained everything. You didn't say no to guys like Brody.

Winston turned to Sophie, blushing. "He also brags that he drove you crazy. You probably shouldn't have told everybody that you wouldn't kiss him back."

"I'll do what I want, thank you," Sophie answered.

"Okay. But, yeah. I told you. Jerk," Winston grumbled. "He says stuff about how someone's eyebrows can make them not in the top ten, or someone's toes can make them not on the list and stuff."

"*What*?" Nessa smacked her own forehead. "A girl's *toes*? Let's get a look at *his* toes, huh?"

"That's so stupid," Eve added.

"It's all stupid!" Winston turned away from them and hit the top of the piano, just like Sophie had the night of the assembly, she remembered. "And even when the guys don't agree with him, or don't care, they just say 'yeah, you're right' to whatever he says. My best friend . . . Well, my *ex*–best friend, Caleb, he just listens and laughs and is like 'totally, man.'"

Sophie had never heard a boy say "ex–best friend" before.

"Wait." Sophie turned to the girls. "How can we trust him?" She pointed at Winston.

"You can!" he pleaded, taking a step toward them.

Sophie shushed him. "Seriously, he's Brody's friend."

"Hmm. She's not wrong." Nessa crossed her arms just like Sophie.

"Have you guys seen me with him the past couple weeks?"

Sophie hadn't, now that she thought about it. He sat with them at lunch . . . well, not for the past week. And she didn't see him in the halls, except with Caleb, sometimes.

"Okay, I haven't. But why?" she challenged him.

Winston sighed and held a palm to his forehead as if he had a headache. "Because I don't like them anymore, okay? And I just—"

"You want to leave the Empire and join the Jedis?" Nessa interrupted.

"Yeah," Winston answered. "That's right."

Sophie wasn't entirely convinced. But it was true that without him and his inside knowledge, they had nothing on Brody at all.

Nessa and Eve turned to Sophie, as if she was the deciding vote on whether to let him stay or not.

Sophie surrendered. "So you'll help us, then," she said.

"Wait, with what?" Nessa asked. "What else is there to do?"

"Before tonight, we didn't know for *sure* that Brody did this. And we also only thought about getting him caught. Punished. After tonight . . ." Sophie felt the thoughts that had stirred inside her, unnamed, form themselves. "We *know* he did it. We were right all along! Right, Winston?"

Winston nodded.

"And we can't just bring him to Principal Yu. No. That's not enough. He needs to be"—she took a breath and decided Brody's fate—"*humiliated*. He needs to be so humiliated that no one ever cares what he thinks again. Not one, single girl."

"Or boy," Winston added.

He was right. "Or boy," she repeated.

Winston took a seat next to them.

"It can't just be about finding proof of his crimes," Sophie thought out loud. "It's got to be more than that. We have to find undeniable proof that makes the school hate him. Proof that could get him *expelled*."

"You're right," Nessa agreed. "Nobody's safe with him around."

"Exactly. We have to expose him," Sophie went on. "In front of *everyone*." She turned to Nessa, knowing she would understand.

"The show!" Nessa lit up.

"Huh?" Eve's face scrunched up in confusion.

"Yes! We have to expose him at the show!" Sophie almost hugged Nessa. This was genius.

Nessa jumped up and down a little. "Final curtain call! Tell everyone everything we find!"

"Yes!" Sophie found herself holding hands with Nessa and jumping a couple of times with her. Then she went into planning mode.

Winston was a science guy, so she instructed him to find out the IP address of LordTesla. That could potentially break the whole case. Winston told her he didn't know that much about computers, but she shrugged him off. He'd do fine. Nessa had the job of not only spying on Brody all the way through rehearsal, just like she had before, but also finding a time to secretly go through his backpack. They had to push harder in every way to catch a guy like him. To Sophie's chagrin, Nessa insisted that Sophie do makeup and costumes so that she could help, too. Sophie relented. Fine. She'd be a theater kid for a little bit. She wasn't going back to the Sophies, anyway.

"What about me?" Eve asked as Sophie gave out the tasks.

Sophie didn't know. Eve would be a pariah on Monday. She'd rejected Brody, just like Sophie had.

"I'll think of something," Sophie assured her.

"I also think we need more girls," Nessa said. "All eyes need to be on him in rehearsal, from all corners. What if he tries something like what he did tonight?"

Nessa was right. "Who can we trust?" Sophie asked.

"I have some ideas." Nessa smiled. "I'm on it."

"You guys are some serious vigilantes," Winston muttered. "I'm impressed."

Eve laughed in recognition, but Sophie had no idea what he meant. "We're what?"

"Vigilantes," Eve explained. "It means when the law isn't doing its job, you do it yourself."

"Yeah." Winston jumped onto her explanation, like they could read each other's thoughts. "A good example would be Batman."

"Or," Eve continued, "in real life, in about the early 1900s—"

"I like it," Sophie said, cutting them off.

"I think we've got the name of our little group here!" Nessa declared.

"What? The Vigilantes?" Eve asked, incredulous.

"No. The Dark Knights," Nessa explained, as if such a leap were obvious.

"A knight is usually a boy. No, thank you. Not for this group," Sophie asserted.

"Okay, fine." Nessa pulled out her phone and spoke into it. "What's the name for a female knight?"

Her phone answered in its robot voice: "A female Viking warrior is called a Shieldmaiden."

"Yes!" Nessa and Sophie squealed.

"Vikings?" Winston questioned. "When did we ask about Vikings?"

"I'll take it," Sophie said. They were Shieldmaidens, going to war for the sake of eighth grade girls everywhere. Or at least at Ford.

"Changing the chat name right now and adding Winston!" Nessa hummed to herself as she fiddled with her phone.

The sounds of the dance down the hall drifted under the slit of the choir room door.

"Worst dance ever, right?" Winston said to all of them as he leaned his back against the piano.

"Winston, you have bad friends. I can relate," Sophie said.

Nessa hopped over to the piano, and a few notes floated into the room. "Let's make our own dance." And Nessa began to sing. Her voice, smooth and pure, made Sophie feel warm all over, like drinking eggnog or eating pumpkin pie, even if the song sounded a century old.

As Nessa crooned, Sophie saw Winston slip his Green Hornet mask onto Eve's face.

Eve grinned.

"Hey. Even if they stare, with this on they won't be able to really see you," she heard Winston say.

"*I'd rather be blue over you . . . ,*" Nessa sang.

Sophie hopped up and grabbed Eve's and Winston's hands. They put their arms around one another and swayed side to side.

Eve moved just as awkwardly as she had in her bedroom a month earlier.

At the memory, a huge laugh burst out of Sophie. "Eve Hoffman, I'll say this about you," Sophie said, feeling lighter than she had in a long time. "When I'm with you, I end up dancing. I don't know why."

Sophie grabbed Eve's hands and they spun and she let the world outside the room drift away. Now that everyone knew about her, or maybe admitted what they'd always known, that she didn't *actually* fit in at all, the world she'd be returning to in the hallways would be a very different one. A world she didn't yet know how to conquer.

30

EVE

They must have known she could hear them.

They spoke lowly, but not in whispers.

Looking up and down the hallways, Eve swore that everyone's eyes glowed red, like demons'. Even the hall monitors and teachers seemed to look at her differently. Did they *all* know about Brody's accusation at the dance?

On Monday afternoon, as she walked by the science lab, she heard Curtis Milford say to a friend, "I *told* you she wrote it, dude. Just *look* at her. Yuck."

Principal Yu approached her to find a time they could

talk. She probably believed Eve wrote the list, too. Eve made up an excuse and escaped.

Tuesday morning, when she entered homeroom, Miranda Garland muttered to those who sat behind her, "Did you know she's *Jewish*?"

"What? Really?" someone asked in shock, like Miranda had told them Eve was secretly half-human, half-crab.

Eve clenched her palm around her hamsa necklace and kept her head down.

During PE on Wednesday, as they did laps, she saw a group of boys making fun of her chest. She told Ms. Meijer she felt nauseous, and she headed to the nurse's office to lie down.

As she lay on the office's cot, she heard her phone buzz. She didn't need to check it. She knew what it said. The texts when she'd been "the prettiest" hadn't been great, but now that she was the school's lying fraud, they were much worse.

How could a person be so stuck-up?

Pathetic

U didn't fool me who could believe u would be no 1

You're a _____

You're a _____

You're a _____

Fill in the blank. It went on and on.

They could all think and say whatever they wanted. They could hate her and call her names. Eve could take on all the venom that the school spat out. Maybe she deserved it. She'd stayed silent when the Sophies had called Sophie "pathetic," and when Brody claimed Sophie was "crazy." She hadn't said a thing when Brody told her Nessa didn't "fit the part."

How ironic that her mom had always said, with a twinkle in her eye, that she'd named Eve after "not just the first woman, but the first *rebel*."

Eve wouldn't remain quiet again. She'd find a way to speak out. Somehow.

She pulled her notebook out of her backpack and tried to do a poetry exercise. Shut out the noise. Just shut out the world. It had worked during the October assembly.

What was a poem she knew well?

Maybe a line from one of her new favorites, one she'd found in her hours spent clicking on random poems online: "The Cloud" by Percy Shelley.

I am the daughter of Earth and Water, And the nursling of the Sky . . .

I am the daughter of . . ., she wrote. And all she could think of was her mother's name. Deb. *I am the daughter of Deb*. Deb and Joe. What could be less poetic?

So she started two words back. *I am . . . I am . . .* Usually her mind came up with something, even if she later recognized it wasn't very good. But now . . . it was like her mind had gone as blank as a snowy field.

All weekend, since the Halloween dance, even with her notebooks and Emily Dickinson surrounding her, she'd had no words.

All she could hear were the voices of what other people said she was. A chorus behind her singing "*liar, fake, phony, yuck.*"

Even though Eve liked to imagine Emily Dickinson's life, and how tranquil and full of beauty it must have been in her room of words and solitude, Eve had to admit that sometimes she mentally glossed over a pretty big part of what she'd read in *All About Emily Dickinson*. Before Emily Dickinson had disappeared into her room forever to write, she'd lived a life out in the world, just like everybody else. A normal life. But then one day, she'd written in a letter to a friend, "I had a terror since September, I could tell to none . . ." And around that time, Emily stopped going outside.

It wasn't some magical devotion to poetry that kept her indoors. It was a "terror." What had that terror been?

As Eve lay in the nurse's office, she wondered if this list had been the start of *her* terror. And for her, the terror took her words away instead of allowing her to write them down.

But she had words for Brody. She dreamed of going back in time, saying to Brody, "Sophie isn't 'crazy.' She never was. She is the sanest person I ever know to have turned you down." And she wanted to say to him, "Nessa has more talent in her finger than you could ever dream of!"

But those moments had passed her by.

Eve got back up and returned to the gym. She didn't have Emily Dickinson's life. There was no safe room to hide in.

On her way out of school that day, she spotted Principal Yu coming toward her in the hall. She pretended not to see her and left the building as fast as she could.

On Friday, Eve arrived at her locker to find LIAR scrawled across it in bright orange spray paint. Briefly, Eve rested her forehead against the locker next to hers and took a breath. She could take this. She could. She straightened herself back up and opened the lock.

"This is vandalism!" Sophie pronounced as she appeared by Eve's side. "I'm getting Principal Yu."

"Don't get involved," Eve said as quietly as possible. "They'll hate you, too."

Eve ignored the spray paint and shoved her coat and backpack into her locker. She heard someone say from behind her, "Look, I've been telling you, it's all tissue in there."

As she turned to see who was talking about her, a sudden shock of cold hit her body. Two eighth graders, a boy and a girl, stood before her as the girl splashed a bottle of water right onto the middle of Eve's chest. She felt the water drip down her stomach and onto the floor.

Sophie hollered something at them as they scurried off, their laughter echoing down the hall.

At the start of her next class, Eve's social studies teacher informed her she'd been summoned by Principal Yu.

Eve could no longer avoid her.

"Eve, come on in." Principal Yu welcomed her into an office dressed up as a greenhouse. Plants hung from the walls and sat in the sunny windowsills. A row of succulents lined her desk.

Eve sat down and fixed her eyes on the plants. "Hi."

"What happened to your shirt?" Principal Yu asked.

"Just clumsy. Spilled my water bottle."

"I see." Principal Yu paused. "I'm sorry you have to miss social studies for this. But maybe *you're* not," she joked.

Eve couldn't politely pretend to laugh like she might have two months before.

"How are you, Eve?" Principal Yu sounded casual.

Was she going to expel her now, for writing the list?

"Fine," Eve answered.

"Hmm."

Eve, still staring at the plump green leaves, sensed Principal Yu nodding.

"Your parents say they've noticed some changes in you recently," Principal Yu said. "As have I."

Huh? Her parents? Eve looked up. "They talked to you?"

"A bit," Principal Yu said like it was no big deal.

How embarrassing! Why would they do that?

"They said there have been some new friends in your life lately, and that you've been wearing some makeup, dressing differently."

During the Brody days, Eve had put on her makeup in the bathroom at school and taken it off with wet tissue before she got home. Apparently it hadn't fooled them.

"And now," Principal Yu went on, "it seems you've had a tough week. It *has* been a difficult few days, yes?"

Eve bit the insides of her cheeks. "Ha. Few days . . ."

"I can imagine that being number one on that appalling list was hard for you."

Eve swallowed. "Yes."

"It would be too much for anybody."

Eve thought of Sophie, how much she had wanted that

kind of thing for herself. Would it have been too much for Sophie, too?

"Truly. Anybody. Even if they don't know it," Principal Yu said as if reading Eve's thoughts.

"Wait, so this isn't about the spray paint on my locker?" Eve looked up. She saw that Principal Yu looked a bit sad herself.

"Well, not entirely," Principal Yu answered.

"And this isn't about you thinking I wrote the list?"

"No." Principal Yu shook her head emphatically. "No, I don't believe you did it."

"Wait." Eve shifted in her seat and leaned in toward the desk. "Maybe that's a problem, Principal Yu. Maybe you *should* suspect me. Because this all should have been investigated right away. Every claim should be taken seriously." All her fury about how long this had been going on began to come out. "Why has no one gotten in trouble for all this? Sophie Kane lost her friends! Winston Byrd, too! Girls are crying in bathrooms! And adults don't do anything!"

Principal Yu said nothing.

"And is this seriously the first time you're trying to talk to me about it? Did you think I was happy before, like it was some 'compliment,' like my dad did? What is wrong with you all?"

"We offered counselors, Eve. We can't force you to speak to us," Principal Yu responded calmly.

"No! No." Eve felt her hands turn to fists on her lap. "You should have helped."

Principal Yu allowed a moment of quiet to go by. The corners of her mouth turned up slightly. "I assure you, we have investigated every claim thoroughly."

"Oh, really?" An angry voice came out of Eve that she didn't recognize. "Then why isn't it all over yet?"

"We've conducted several interviews with students, and we do think we have an idea, but we can't make anything public until we're certain, Eve," Principal Yu said with a quiet confidence that stopped Eve from saying anything more.

"Okay," Eve said. "I'm sorry."

"And Eve, I do wish we'd called you in to talk to the counselor. We didn't want any girl to feel unfairly targeted for counseling due to that particular individual's"—she paused as if to think of the right word—"position on the list. I wish . . ." Principal Yu sighed. "I wish I'd known better what to do."

Eve didn't know what to say.

"When I was in eighth grade," Principal Yu said slowly, "I remember . . ." She paused. "There was this boy, Wes. He had short, bleached hair."

"What?" Eve couldn't imagine any of the guys in school with bleached hair.

"Yup. That was the style then."

"Wow."

"An unfortunate period." Principal Yu laughed and then paused again. "Wes wouldn't stop grabbing me. And snapping my bra."

Eve tried to picture Principal Yu as an eighth grader. She was tiny now, so she was probably tiny then. She had kind, delicate features with eyebrows in a permanent state of listening-face.

"He thought it was hysterical. And I told him 'Ow!' I told him to stop. I probably used foul language of some sort."

Eve could *not* imagine Principal Yu cursing. She was so put together, so classy.

"And I told the school counselor. She was nice, but ineffective. I think she thought that what Wes was doing to me was just . . . normal. And I think, to her, normal meant okay. Well, one day, Wes snapped my bra so hard that I got a small cut in the back from the metal of the clasp." She reached toward her back as if to point to it. "I bled through my shirt."

Eve instinctively covered her mouth. "Oh my gosh! What did they do to him?"

Principal Yu tapped her fingers on the edge of her desk and sighed. "Nothing."

"Oh." Eve wished she had something smart or kind to say. "Did you do anything? Did you say anything to him?"

Principal Yu shrugged. "No. I wish I had, though."

It was hard to know what to say. Hard to see how to make it all stop.

"We're getting your locker cleaned off as we speak," Principal Yu said. "And we won't stop looking for answers."

Eve glanced toward the door and back to Principal Yu, unsure if she could go or not.

"You can head back to class now," Principal Yu told Eve. "And Eve? You can come to me with anything, okay? Anything."

Eve nodded. Before she left she turned back to Principal Yu and said, "Wes shouldn't have gotten away with it."

"You're right," Principal Yu answered.

As Eve headed past her ruined locker, she saw Mr. Glaze, the school custodian, scrubbing off the paint. And, to her utter surprise, Winston Byrd stood alongside him, holding a sponge. He lifted a hand to acknowledge her and then returned to removing the orange stain.

31

NESSA

"Hey, Lara! Wait up!" Nessa caught Lara in the hallway.

"What's the story?" Lara usually responded with this greeting. And as other people spoke, she always played with her array of colorful bracelets, creating a jingly background in all conversations.

Nessa gave Lara her pitch. "Still mad you're not on the list even though you're obviously fabulous? Mad there's a list at all? Well, have I got an answer for you."

"This is a strange infomercial," Lara answered. Jingle, jingle.

"I'll cut to the chase."

"Thanks."

"We know that Brody Dixon wrote the list. We have a witness. And Brody has been bullying girl after girl after girl, and"—Nessa eyed the people around them—"and we are going to find proof that he did it and show it to a packed crowd at final curtain call of *The Music Man*. We need all awesome girl hands on deck. You in?"

"Um." Lara put a finger up in the air. "Reminder. Your best friend wrote the list."

"No, she didn't."

"And no one cares about the list anymore, because we're all just mad at her." Lara turned to walk away, and Nessa grabbed her arm.

"Why do you believe him and not her?" No answer. "Why?"

Lara paused. "Well . . ." She seemed to truly think about it. "Eve hasn't said anything to defend herself."

"What would she say?"

"She could say *something*."

"What?"

Lara just stared at her. She had nothing.

"And if she did say something, you'd believe her then?" Nessa went on.

Lara raised one eyebrow in a very cool move that Nessa envied.

"I wish I could do that," Nessa admitted.

"Okay." Lara gave in. "Tell me more."

32

EVE

After school, Eve tossed all the clothes Sophie had picked for her into the back of her closet in a pile.

It was time to make a change. Not just for her friends, but for herself. For everybody. Just because something was normal didn't mean it was okay.

Eve remembered Winston's words at the Halloween dance as he'd put a mask over her eyes: *Even if they stare, with this on they won't be able to really see you.*

Eve didn't want to hide anymore. Not inside her brother's big shirts. Not in the nurse's office. But she also didn't want to allow anyone to stare at her like her face and body were open for judgment.

When people looked her way, she'd give them something to think about. She'd be the one in charge. She'd send them all a message: *Back. Off.*

Hey, Eve texted Winston, whose number she'd grabbed from the Shieldmaidens chat, **Thank you for earlier.**

After a moment he responded, **pls dont mention it.**

How'd you get out of class? she asked.

Ha. Science class. All I'm doing is extra credit stuff, anyway. Not trying to brag. Just really easy for me. So Miss Melvin didn't mind if I left.

She had something important to ask him, and she got right to it. **Hey, so . . . ,** she wrote, **do you still have that Green Hornet mask? Could I borrow it?**

33

NESSA

Lara and Erin are in! Nessa wrote to the group that night.

Nessa had hooked Erin O'Brien so easily at rehearsal. Two words into her sell and Erin had said, "I will do anything to help you take down that nitwit. Just say the word."

Ugh, fine, Sophie responded to Nessa's text.

Power in numbers! Nessa wrote back.

But minutes later, Sophie called her. An actual call. On the phone.

Nessa picked up and said, stunned, "Hel*lo*?"

"I don't trust these girls."

"Hello to you, too."

"Lara most likely hates me. Remember how people hate me?"

Nessa did remember, because she hadn't been Sophie's biggest fan, either.

Right on cue, Sophie added, "You hated me. Maybe you still do."

"I don't hate you."

Sophie didn't respond. Nessa could hear TV playing loudly in the background and a little girl's voice chattering away. Way too many seconds of not-talking went by.

"Do you watch *Dance House*?" Nessa asked.

"Of *course* I do! Go Teeny, right?"

"No! Teeny's the worst!" Wow. How could Sophie like hair-puller Teeny?

"Teeny's doing what she needs to do to win the show!" Sophie argued.

"Teeny's ruining it for everybody else," Nessa shot back.

They debated every dancer on the show's three-year history.

"Hey, wait." Nessa stopped Sophie in the middle of her rant about unfair judging. "You think I never liked you. But you treated me like I was see-through until, like, two seconds ago."

No answer from Sophie.

"You didn't talk to me," Nessa went on. "What was I supposed to think about you?"

The TV continued to blare in the background.

"Yeah, maybe," Sophie answered after a beat. "Fair point."

Nessa hadn't expected that response. "Hey. I think it's really awesome that you didn't kiss Brody, by the way," Nessa told her. She'd been meaning to say this, at some point. "You shouldn't have done something you didn't want to do."

Another moment of silence passed by on Sophie's end of the line. Then, abruptly, Sophie said, "Thanks. Anyway, I should go. Talk later."

When Nessa turned out her light that night, her phone glowed with a text from Sophie to the new Shieldmaidens:
Welcome to the team.

34

EVE

The green of the mask surrounding her brown eyes made her think of a forest.

Eve got the mask from Winston in school that Monday morning, and that night she took it out of the front pocket of her backpack where it had lain tucked away all day. She slipped it on her face, and texted him a selfie of her wearing it.

I'm never taking it off, she wrote to him.

lol awesome, he wrote back. And then a minute later, more words popped up: **I know what it's like to want**

to hide, too, trust me. thats how i spent like all of elementary school

She didn't know how to respond so she texted back a smiley face emoji.

But Eve wasn't hiding. She was fighting back.

35

NESSA

Early that week, Brody came back to school.

And by then, the school's ecosystem had been rearranged.

Eve was still famous, after years of being a nobody, but she wasn't famous for being the new prettiest anymore. She was known as a monster.

A monster with a mask. Eve had come to school wearing Winston's Green Hornet mask from Halloween. Nessa had tried to tell Eve that if she didn't want to be stared at, a green mask with a little wasp on it wasn't the way to go.

What was even weirder was that Eve had left a few superhero masks out in the bathroom and on tables in the cafeteria and now a couple of other girls were wearing them, too. More than a couple. So strange.

And the Sophies were officially no longer the Sophies because Sophie had left them. Rose Reed now sat in the middle of the Sophies' table. Even Amina, who'd been higher on the list, seemed to follow Rose's lead. They all wore pink belts.

And Sophie had solidified a new look: *happy*. She seemed to laugh a lot more. Especially at things Nessa said, which Nessa had to admit she liked. Sometimes, Sophie even dressed for track practice before it began.

The new Sophie Kane sat with Nessa, Eve, Lara, Erin, and Winston.

Winston no longer spoke to Brody. And he'd stopped speaking to his "ex–best friend" Caleb, as far as Nessa could tell. But Nessa saw Winston glare at Caleb from across the room sometimes. And Caleb glared right back.

Nessa tried to imagine how that could happen to a pair of best friends. What if Eve changed so much one day that they couldn't even stand each other anymore? It sounded impossible. But Eve *had* been very different lately. First the whole brunette bombshell thing, and recently those masks. Nessa felt her moving further and further away.

"Evie, you planning on taking that thing off one of these days?" Nessa asked her at lunch.

Eve gave her a tight smile. "Nope."

"It makes you look kinda . . . twisted."

Eve shrugged. "Oh well."

"And haven't you gotten into trouble for it at school?" Nessa marveled.

"So? What can they do about it?"

That *definitely* didn't sound like the Evie she knew. "Moving on . . ." Nessa changed the subject. "Any updates on the tech side of things, Byrd?"

"Um, no."

"I don't think your science genius brain is doing enough for us here with LordTesla's IP address. You need to help in another way, too. Do lights for the show. Get involved with the sixth grader working the switchboard. He's a disaster. Mr. Rhodes is so frustrated."

"Um, I—I—"

"No choice. It's a rule of the Shieldmaidens."

A group of Sophie's old friends walked by them, headed toward the cafeteria door, and they whispered as they passed by. Amina Alvi stopped at their table and stood in front of Sophie.

"Hey, Sophie," Amina said. "We miss you at our table."

Sophie kept her eyes down on her lunch and raised a hand to signal hello without looking up at all.

“Okay, cool!” Amina’s tone was breezy, as if nothing was awkward at all. “See ya!” She followed the other girls out.

“Soph, we may need a Sophie—I mean a Rose—to make sure the other kids come to the show?” Nessa reminded her. “Maybe you could get Amina on board with us?”

“Brody is the *lead*,” Sophie snapped, in a way Nessa hadn’t heard since before the dance. “The little sheep will be there to see him, anyway.”

“Yeah, but . . .” Lara looked at Nessa and Winston for permission to go on. She still seemed a little scared of Sophie. “We need Rose and those girls there on the right night, when we expose him. If they all come the first night, it won’t work.”

Eve broke her silence. “None of this means anything because we don’t have evidence. And until we do? I’m the bad guy in school. Not him.” She picked up her backpack and left the cafeteria. “Take one,” she said as she tossed a few of her masks onto the table.

Eve had a point.

One night after dinner, as Nessa and the Shieldmaidens tried to guess Brody’s email password, Nessa’s dad knocked on her door.

“One sec!” she yelled out as she wrote some good ones: **MONEYBAGS, TONEDEAF123?**

As she giggled away, her dad opened the door and came in.

"Honey," he began. Uh-oh. "Honey" meant a talk was coming.

"Dad, I'm really busy."

"Weak attempt," her dad said, making her laugh.

She put the phone down.

"I'll cut to the chase," he said. "The word on the street is that Evie wrote the list."

Nessa rolled her eyes. Even her parents thought Eve was a liar? "First of all, don't ever say 'word on the street' again, and second of all, how could you ever think that—"

"I don't, I don't," he assured her. Her dad scooted next to her on the bed and ran a hand through her hair. It made her feel about eight years old, but she liked it. "I'm sure Principal Yu doesn't, either."

"You never know," Nessa grumbled. "All the kids think she did it."

"I'm sure. And I know this year hasn't been great so far for her, or probably for you?" He gave her a questioning look, but she said nothing. "But just remember," her dad recited his usual phrase, "This, too, shall—"

"Pass," she finished for him.

But it didn't quite comfort her this time.

"But, Dad," she began, speaking slowly so as to say exactly

what she meant, "before 'it' passes, what are we supposed to do about it? You have to *do* something when life is hard, when people get hurt."

"That is the question," he said. He thought for a minute. "Love yourself," he said. "Love others. Be kind. And remember how strong you are." He squeezed her knee. "I hope that for Evie, too."

"Evie has no idea just how strong she is." Nessa laid her head on her pillows.

"She will one day." Her dad got up. He leaned over, kissed her forehead, and headed to the door. "Oh yeah." He turned back around. "You know some other wisdom I like?"

"What?"

"'Father, forgive them; for they know not what they do.'"

With that, he shut the door.

Nessa wasn't so sure about that one, either. Sometimes it seemed like they knew exactly what they did.

And look what they'd done to Eve.

36

EVE

A few more girls started to wear the masks. Eve and Winston had biked to the dollar store and picked up packs and packs of them.

"You're my trusted accomplice," she'd told him.

"Your Kato, if you will," he'd answered, informing her that Kato was Green Hornet's brilliant sidekick.

That next morning at school, Winston had reached into his back pocket and pulled out a mask of his own. "Feel the sting of the Green Hornet," he said as he slipped it on his face. Then he added, "Green Hornet catchphrase," before trotting off to class.

Eve left the masks on hallway window ledges all over the school.

"So you're trying to convince everyone to deal with bullies by wearing *masks*?" Nessa asked her once.

Nessa had seemed annoyed about the masks from the very first day that Eve wore one. What Nessa didn't seem to comprehend was how *free* Eve felt with the mask on. Instead of wondering what each person thought about her, or what each person wanted from her, or if a given person would text her something awful later, she could look all of them in the eye and silently say to them: *I'm no longer in the running for your lists or comments or judgments*. The mask screamed out, "*Whatever you thought I was, you were wrong. You don't know me at all.*"

She tried to write this explanation out to Nessa, but Nessa just texted her back:

o why didn't I think of that all the times anyone made fun of me.

o yea that's right. cuz it wouldn't have helped me AT ALL.

Eve planned on apologizing to Nessa the next day, but she didn't know what to say sorry for. So instead, she just let Nessa be frustrated with her.

Then one day, Eve saw a seventh grader wearing one of the masks.

"Hey, take that off!" a teacher scolded the girl.

The seventh grader pulled it off, but as the teacher moved away, she put it right back on. As she walked by Eve, the girl held her hand out for a high five.

Under her mask, Eve's eyes crinkled in a smile.

If Nessa could have seen that, maybe she would have changed her mind.

Abe had just passed his driver's test, and he'd spent the past twenty-four hours convincing their parents that if the law said he could drive, then who were they to say he couldn't pick up his sisters from school?

"We're nervous parents, okay?" his mom had said.

"Not a reasonable argument!" he'd fought back.

Eventually, they'd relented.

"Hi!" he practically sang as Eve got into the car.

"Hey."

"Okay, we have like half an hour before Hannah gets out. So I need you to tell me what's going on, Britt Reid."

"Who?"

"Ha. The Green Hornet's alter ego. You need to read up."

Abe drove them to a spot near an outlet mall down Greer

Road, and they bought hot chocolates. They sat in the car, their drinks steaming, and watched passersby go in and out of shops.

"Isn't it wild that tomorrow we're celebrating a holiday *with* the rest of the kids in town?"

"Yeah, actually," she said. "I never really thought of it that way."

They missed so many days of school for their holidays in the fall, and had to spend tons of time catching up on schoolwork, but on Thanksgiving everyone else went home, too. Weird.

"So, how's the whole being-called-the-prettiest-girl-in-eighth-grade thing going?" he asked.

"Did Mom and Dad ask you to talk to me?" Eve scowled at him. "God, they're involving the whole world in my life!"

"Mom just worries!" He sounded so much like their dad that they looked at each other for a moment and then broke out into laughter. It felt good to laugh like that with him again. It was almost like they were back in one of their pillow forts playing cards.

"So really, though," he went on as their giggles died down, "what's going on?"

Eve told him. Well, she told him the most important bits—the makeover, Brody's horrible costume, the so-far fruitless plan to expose him, everyone saying she wrote the list, and why she initially put on the mask.

"So other people are wearing the masks, too?"

"Yeah. Even my guy friend, actually."

"Oh yeah? So this guy is wearing his mask in solidarity with you, huh? Cool."

"Yeah?" she answered, unsure.

Abe smiled. "It's very cool he's willing to join ranks with the girls and that he's on your side; that he's supporting you."

She thought of how the morning after she'd texted Winston, he'd brought his Halloween mask to school for her. The way he smacked his lips in concentration as he scrubbed the paint off her locker. His grin as he put on the Green Hornet mask.

"Yeah, he's on my side."

"Sounds like a good guy."

"I think so." Eve took a sip of her drink and felt her body begin to warm.

"And you're making some other friends these days, besides Nessa. Yeah?"

Eve nodded.

But all these questions felt strange. Abe had hardly spoken to her for two years, yet ever since the list had come out, he seemed so invested in her life.

As he started to ask her something else, she interrupted him. "Why do you care so much?"

"What do you mean?"

"You kind of disappeared once high school started. No offense," she added. "And now . . ."

Abe sighed. "Like I said a few weeks back . . . high school is . . ." He focused on their dad's Red Wings keychain hanging from the rearview mirror as if it would give him some answers. "Really different."

"I feel like you're speaking in code," she said.

"Sorry." He took a sip of his drink. "It's just, this whole list thing? Man, it reminded me how middle school can be, like, the *worst*. And you've been going through it all this time, and I . . ." He paused, seeming to search for the right words.

Eve wondered if he even knew that she'd missed talking to him.

"Listen." Abe leaned toward where she sat, pink-faced, in the passenger's seat. "I wasn't always so nice to everybody in middle school. Especially to girls."

Abe? Abe, her big brother? She knew he hadn't always been nice to her and Hannah, pinning them down and pulling their hair and all that, but she couldn't imagine him being like Brody or Caleb or Curtis or the other kids who mocked her and threw water on her chest.

"Really?" Without thinking about it, Eve lifted her mask and let it sit on top of her hair like a headband. "How were you not nice?"

"Lots of ways. Like I laughed at jokes that I knew weren't okay at all." Abe appeared to tighten his grip on his hot chocolate. "Even ones about my own girl friends, sometimes." She saw him shake his head as if he were trying to get rid of a thought.

"Why?"

"I didn't get how much it was hurting them, I think. And I didn't believe that it would matter if I said anything. Like I was . . . *helpless* or something . . . ," he muttered.

"Did you rate them?" Eve asked softly, afraid of the answer.

"No."

Eve began to say "Good," but Abe interjected.

"But I *saw* that kind of stuff and I probably joked about it," he admitted. "Maybe that's why some girls I was friends with back then aren't so eager to hang out with me now." He let out a sad laugh. "Can't really blame them. I didn't stand up for them."

That sounded like *Eve*. Not *Abe*.

"Look." He turned to her. "Not everyone figures out how to be good to other people until way later. *I* didn't. I wish

I could take back the times I just sat there or added some stupid comment I thought was clever while other guys said awful things. I wish I hadn't cared if those guys liked me. But I can't take it back. And I regret it."

Eve thought of Nessa telling her, "This, too, shall pass," on the morning after the list came out.

But some things did stick.

"Did you ever apologize to anyone?" Eve asked him.

Abe thought for a moment and shook his head. "I should have."

The giant inflated turkey in front of the café flapped about in the wind.

"You've found some friends who aren't like I was, though," he said. "Stick with them. And don't put on eyeliner or whatever, or wear that mask, just because of the mean kids. If you want to, that's different. But only make decisions for yourself. Don't let the kids who haven't figured out how to be kind yet get to you so much. Forget 'em. I wasted a lot of time worrying about other people judging me before I figured out it didn't matter. Be better than I was."

Eve looked up at him and saw his earnest smile and pulled the mask back down over her eyes. "You're being cheesy," she said. She buried her face in her palms in embarrassment, and the mask squished up against her skin. It smelled like her mom's lavender oil, which she'd put on the green cloth when it had started to give off the stench of sweat.

Abe chuckled. "Sorry. Had to say it. Now let's go pick up our little sister, who is gonna need a lot more help than either of us, let me tell you." He turned the key in the ignition. "And hey," he added as they pulled out of the parking lot, "you're freaking out Mom and Dad so much with the Green Hornet thing. They might make you start seeing a counselor or something."

"No, they can't be that upset!" Eve insisted. "Really?"

"Not as upset as Mom's gonna be when I tell her I'm an atheist!" Abe swerved out into the street.

Eve almost dropped her drink. "Wha—!"

As they pulled up to the curb at the elementary school, Hannah threw her backpack into the car and groused, "Abe, don't get us killed."

Eve smiled at her little sister.

"What?" Hannah asked, weirded out by the friendliness.

"Nothing," she said. But she felt truly okay for the first time in weeks, like her insides weren't jumbled all about.

After they picked up Hannah and headed home, she texted Winston, **Hey. Thanks for the help today, fellow Hornet.**

37

SOPHIE

Sophie had to admit that she had really taken to the whole makeup-and-costumes thing.

Could she be a Broadway costume designer one day? Or the editor of *Vogue*?

After Sophie's meeting with the tech crew for *The Music Man*, she'd been shocked at their disregard for detail. They were planning on dressing everyone in the same costumes from *Oliver!* the year before, which took place in an entirely different time period and *country*! Sophie told them she'd take over. They could easily piece together costumes from thrift stores in town on a reasonable budget; they just needed to think it through a bit more. Was Sophie the only kid in school who knew how to work on a dang budget? Probably.

After Thanksgiving break, she began working on costumes during rehearsals.

She headed to the library early in December to do some research.

Once she signed in at the library's front desk, she went to the computer section and got to work googling.

In 1912 Iowa, hats looked like UFOs.

Nessa would think that was funny. Sophie would show her pictures later.

Over Thanksgiving break, she'd missed the Shieldmaidens. They wrote on their group chat, sure, but it wasn't the same as being together. She'd never tell them that, but it was true.

She noted with disgust that the girls in 1912 wore bows the size of deep-sea bass. How could they even run and play in those outfits? Early twentieth-century fashion was a disgrace.

The buttons were nice, though. Lots of cute little buttons up and down the front. And she liked the high-waisted skirts. Maybe she'd wear a high-waisted skirt sometime. Clothes and makeup could just be fun. They could be a way of playing around with who you wanted to be or who you already were.

Sophie printed out some photos of looks for the cast, and as she finished up, she dragged the pictures to the trash bin folder on the computer. She went to empty it, but the trash folder was pretty full, with documents dating back all the way to the first week of school, like "Diary Entry of an Ellis Island Immigrant" and "Bio Project—Bill Gates." She saw one doc from Liv Henry, and a part of her wanted to read it and see if Liv was as good at writing as she was. Sophie always felt like she was the best at essays, even if Liv beat her at science and math. But she didn't look. It didn't matter, she told herself. She highlighted her files to delete them, when a Word doc caught her eye. It was dated October 8, 7:23 A.M., and titled "prettiest." Huh?

A part of her knew what she was seeing. A part of her didn't want to know.

Sophie glanced around the library and saw no one but a couple of sixth graders in the fiction section, and the school librarian, Ms. Lyle, going through some papers at her desk.

She clicked on the document and opened it up.

And there it was. Right in front of her. The original list, in tiny type, in rows side by side, perfectly fit together so a phone could take a shot that captured all the names.

Ms. Lyle headed toward the computer section. Sophie pulled out her phone and took a pic of the date and time on the file, as well as a copy of the file's contents, and then emptied the entire trash folder. Anyone could access this computer, and she needed to ensure that *she* was the one with the evidence.

"Need any help back here?" Ms. Lyle asked. Ms. Lyle looked like she'd been working in a library since libraries were invented.

"Nope, I'm good!" Sophie answered in a way-too-peppy voice.

"Oh, lovely." Ms. Lyle continued toward another section of the library, out of sight.

Could Sophie sneak a look at the sign-in book up front before Ms. Lyle returned? She moved pretty slowly, so maybe there was time . . .

If she could get a photo of Brody Dixon's name in the library sign-in at the same time as the Word doc had been written, then he'd be done for. Real evidence! Just the image of the time stamp on the doc and a picture of his name at that exact time and the case for guilt would be made.

Sophie flipped through the pages of the sign-in sheet. October 8 . . . Early morning, before the first period. Who had signed in . . .

And there she saw them—the names of who had come to the library that day and written the list.

No, it couldn't be.

Brody had done it. They knew this.

Had he written another name? Or were these accomplices?

It didn't make sense.

It had to be Brody. It just had to.

Didn't it?

38

EVE

WINSTON: **the cool thing about green hornet is that everyone thinks hes a bad guy, so he gets to infiltrate the bad guys and then stop them. hes this rich guy who owns a newspaper who wants to do good. you know?**

EVE: **A good vigilante**

WINSTON: **yes! exactly! he also has a really cool car. like the batmobile. ha sorry I could talk about this stuff forever. tell me eve stuff**

EVE: **Hmmm. I'm really into poetry these days? Oh my gosh it's so embarrassing**

WINSTON: **no its not! its cool. but im not so good at that kind of stuff.**

i think science is kinda like poetry tho

EVE: **How so?**

WINSTON: **i dunno it sounded smart lol**

EVE: **haha. I mean, they're both about finding answers to things. I think. Or trying to.**

WINSTON: **yeah! and people think theyre hard to understand, but i think once you really get into them, theyre a lot easier than they seem**

EVE: **Sooo true!**

WINSTON: **ok so what's your favorite poem**

EVE: **k I'll send you a link but don't laugh—"The Soul unto itself" by Emily Dickinson**

WINSTON: **ok im not gonna lie i dont get it but ill keep trying**

EVE: **☺ It's ok**

WINSTON: **there was this one famous writer a long time ago who thought of himself as a scientist. august strindberg, have you heard of him?**

I dont think he wrote poems tho

EVE: **What did he discover?**

WINSTON: **nothing. he thought plants had nervous systems so he walked around with a syringe full** of morphine and hed inject apples and stuff to try to prove his theory haha his theory was not correct

fun science fact for you i got lots of em

see this kind of thing is why I got beat up all the time in 5 grade haha

EVE: **So what happened to you back then???**

WINSTON: **I mean I only actually got punched once**

EVE: **What?!?!**

WINSTON: **im really just mad they broke my ornithopter**

EVE: **your huh?**

WINSTON: **sigh. here we go . . . it was this flying contraption made by da vinci?**

so caleb and i worked on this for months, making our own

brought it to school one day

and i guess that was the day a bunch of the other kids decided i was punchable

EVE: **omg!**

WINSTON: **a loser**

they broke the ornithopter and punched me a few times

a piece of my glasses actually sliced under my eye. you can still see the scar

wasnt that bad tho

EVE: it sounds bad!

WINSTON: Caleb stopped them. We grew up on the same block and all that ya know

EVE: that's like me and Nessa

WINSTON: I guess. Except Nessa is still cool

EVE: she's a huge nerd haha like me

WINSTON: I mean she's still nice. Super nice. Caleb is . . . ya know . . .

brodys friend

EVE: I'm sorry. I can't imagine Nessa changing like that. I mean, we're really different and sometimes that's hard, but still

WINSTON: now he just texts rose and watches stupid videos online all day

EVE: ugh I'm sorry

WINSTON: sorry this is probably boring

EVE: it's not! Sometimes I think Nessa thinks I'm. I don't know

WINSTON: what

EVE: too sensitive. She's probably right

WINSTON: **i think its good to be sensitive**

EVE: **maybe. And she can be too NOT sensitive sometimes**

WINSTON: **hey can I see some of your poems?**

EVE: **how'd you know I write my own???**

WINSTON: **I just figured**

EVE: **omg no I don't show anyone**

WINSTON: **please!**

EVE: **maybe . . .**

39

NESSA

Dress rehearsals had sneaked up on them.

December came to Glisgold with several feet of snow and lit-up Santas the size of grizzly bears adorning houses long before Christmas week. And with the constant repetition of Christmas songs in every store came the reality that opening night would soon arrive whether they were ready for it or not.

Nessa was prepared for the show, but not for final curtain call.

She'd gotten *nothing* from Brody. He never left his things out of his sight when she was around. It was easy to think this was because he knew she was Eve's best friend, and he kept his guard up. But that was hard for Nessa to believe, because she'd *always* been invisible to him.

A part of her liked to imagine that Brody was secretly in love with her, but he knew his friends wouldn't accept it, and so he hid his feelings. She knew this was just a fantasy, but there was something about the daydream of him confessing his love to her and her getting to turn him down that she couldn't stop thinking about. During math class, when the teacher went on for too long, she dreamed of rejecting him in front of the whole school. "No, Brody. I just don't feel that way about you!" she'd say, strutting off like they did in the novelas her grandma, a *huge* novelera, watched on Univision.

Sophie had turned down his kiss. Even Eve had gotten a chance to reject him. Some girls had all the luck. *Other* girls.

As tech week got underway, Nessa, Lara, and Erin tried multiple times to create a diversion and get Brody distracted enough that one of them could search through his things. Lara and Erin even pretended to get into a huge fight over a made-up boyfriend living in Finland. Nessa thought they were pretty convincing, and worried slightly that Erin might go overboard and slap Lara. But instead of luring Brody away from his backpack, they just annoyed

Mr. Rhodes with their hollering and elicited nothing but a chuckle from Brody.

As opening night neared, Nessa almost lost hope. But then, one day, a Christmas miracle occurred.

The weather demanded winter coats, and often the cast would throw theirs in a pile in the corner of the auditorium. Two days before the show, all the other kids had left rehearsals after a run-through, and Mr. Rhodes asked Brody and Nessa to stay behind to work on their song. This happened a lot because, of course, Brody couldn't find his note with a pitch pipe implanted in his brain. When they finished up, Mr. Rhodes spoke to Brody for a second and Nessa, being the excellent citizen that she was, picked up both of their coats and went to hand Brody his navy blue Patagonia. Walking toward the piano, as she held it out to him, she spotted orange paint stains surrounding the inner pocket. Stains the *exact* shade of the orange paint sprayed onto Eve's locker.

The markings of a vandal.

Brody hadn't been in school the week that happened, so Nessa hadn't even suspected him. Had he sneaked in after hours? Or been allowed to go to sports practice? Somehow, he had found time to be even more of a jerk to Eve. Nessa almost laughed. Brody had thought he'd get away with it. But now, finally, she had him. He could get *expelled.*

As Brody sang, Nessa laid his coat down on the chair and pulled out her phone.

Nessa saw him look at her. And he saw her take a picture and slip that evidence into her pocket.

"Nessa, mind joining in on this harmony one more time before you go?" Mr. Rhodes asked.

"Sure," she answered with a grin.

As Brody and Nessa crooned a love song together, their hands cradling each other's, his breath surprisingly minty, Nessa let herself believe that he was Harold Hill, and she felt pleased as he hit his high notes with some accuracy, and for a brief moment she let go of the reality that both of them knew that she would be the one to take him down.

40

EVE

EVE: **Okay so I've never shown this stuff to ANYBODY before, okay???**

WINSTON: **It's okay! I'm not going to judge you or something. hey I can show you my ornithopter lol I recreated it after they broke it**

EVE: **The da vinci thing? Haha. I don't know what it is but I'd love that**

WINSTON: **Just kidding. You don't have to show me, seriously. But id love to see some if you change your mind.**

EVE: **Aaah okay I'll show you some. It's all just**

scribbles really and most of it's bad. I just started writing this summer. It's stupid and it doesn't rhyme

WINSTON: **don't worry just send it!**

EVE: **Okay. Okay I'm sending you some. Here goes . . .**

41

SOPHIE

Brody must have used someone else's name to sign into the library that morning. He was a smart-ish guy. He might have planned it all out with that much detail. He must have known that the administrators would look into it, right? So he signed in with a different name.

Unless . . .

No, it had to be Brody. That's why he falsely accused Eve of writing the list! He was *horrible*! And he had tortured every girl in the school at one point or another. Maybe that's why more and more of them wore the masks that Eve scattered around everywhere.

When Nessa texted the Shieldmaidens to tell them she had evidence that Brody had spray painted Eve's locker, Sophie hadn't mentioned what she'd seen in the library.

Something in her told her not to.

And with proof of vandalism, the Shieldmaidens finally had something for their closing night reveal.

A plan had been formulated. Sophie would sew a pocket into Nessa's costume at final dress that night. For her last scene, they'd slip a cell phone inside it. Lara and Erin would block Brody's exits so he couldn't run offstage. Winston would prep Nessa's phone so that as the bows came to a close, she could just press send, shooting the image of Brody's coat with the orange stains, along with the image of Eve's locker, to every phone number and email in the student body. Across the image it would read, "*Why would an innocent person do this*?"

But what if Brody got in trouble for the spray painting, and then the administration looked into him more closely and found the library sign-in? Sophie had deleted the Word doc, she reminded herself, so she was the only one with the photos. And Winston said Brody had bragged about it. Why would he brag about it if he hadn't written it himself? It was him, she told herself, and he deserved whatever he got.

He'd called her "white trash." He'd said she had *fleas*.

And all because of a pair of puckered lips and a turn of the head.

As Sophie headed to rehearsal that afternoon, Amina Alvi walked toward her. Sophie was the only other person in the hallway. She pretended to look up at something on the ceiling, as if the water-stained tiles were as fascinating as the constellations in the night sky. When that became ridiculous, she began to peek inside each classroom she passed, like she was looking for someone. Anything to avoid eye contact with the girl who had betrayed her in a stairwell—so tacky—and who was now following Rose without a thought as to how Sophie might be doing.

But as they crossed each other's paths, Amina spoke.

"Hey," she said.

Sophie gave a nod but kept her gaze averted and walked on.

"Hey, can I talk to you for a second?"

"Fine," Sophie answered.

"We haven't talked much lately, huh?" Amina let out a nervous, breathy giggle.

"Yup." Sophie transformed her face to ice and stone. She gripped the straps of her backpack.

"You don't sit with us anymore." Amina took a step closer to Sophie.

"Um, yeah, ya think?" Sophie couldn't make herself pretend it was nothing, or keep her mouth shut. It was too exhausting. "I heard you talking about me in the stairwell. The day after the list came out. Right before the parent meeting." She locked her stern eyes with Amina's. "And things just got worse from there."

"What?" Amina looked flustered. "I never talked about you! I stand up for you all the time!"

Sophie scoffed. "Oh, so that means people are talking about me all the time?" Of course they were. "Anyway, that's not the point. I *heard* you."

"What do you think I said? I didn't say anything!" Amina looked like she might cry.

Sophie tried to remember exactly what Amina had said, but she couldn't recall who said what anymore. "You were all saying how I'm not really pretty. And Eve is. Rose is. It's obvious you all truly felt that because look at who you're following now."

"Following?" Amina said. "What do you mean by that?"

"Oh, come on. Rose." Sophie felt herself crossing her arms, not letting Amina in.

"I don't know what you mean by 'following' Rose. You left our table. Rose was still there. What was I *supposed* to do? You obviously didn't want to be friends anymore."

"We were never friends," Sophie spat back.

They heard a door shut in the hallway, and two teachers walked past them, chatting.

"Hi, girls," one of them said. The other waved.

"Hi, Ms. Tilo!" Amina singsonged. She'd always been every teacher's favorite. Probably because she knew how to act really nice.

When the teachers were a few yards away, Amina's smile disappeared. Her face crumpled.

"We *were* friends." Amina's voice broke. She wiped a tear away, and Sophie could see her try to hold more back.

"Were we?" Sophie's arms dropped. "Then why didn't we . . . I don't know, talk about stuff? Why didn't you ever stand up for me when the list came out? Why didn't you come after me at the Halloween dance? Seriously!"

"I know, it was really bad what Brody did to you!" Amina countered. "I'm really sorry, okay? I didn't have any friends until you came to school halfway through sixth grade. I just studied, and felt weird all the time. And *nobody* here looked like me. Do you have *any* idea how that feels?"

"No," Sophie acknowledged. She didn't.

"I sat all alone at lunch. And then there was you. I couldn't believe you wanted to be my friend."

"Oh." Sophie leaned against a locker and felt her shoulders droop.

Amina slouched, pressing her shoulder against the locker next to her. "But, sorry, you just . . . you never really talked about yourself. I didn't want to ask the wrong questions. You got pretty mad when I did."

"Oh!" Sophie repeated. She couldn't believe what she was hearing, but at the same time she knew it was true. She hated when Amina or Liv or Hayley got nosy.

"Sorry for being a bad friend." Amina began to cry again.

They stood there for a minute or so, and watched as a couple of boys walked by, staring at them, followed by a group of girls in superhero masks.

"Hey," Sophie said. "Didn't Brody like you before he liked me?"

Amina nodded, sniffling.

"What happened?"

Amina laughed. "Oh, you don't even want to know."

"No, I really do," Sophie told her.

They walked toward the auditorium together as Amina told Sophie how Brody had come on really strong, and

Amina's parents didn't let her go to boys' houses, and how Brody had said that was really stupid, and after asking her a bunch of times and hearing her say no just as many times, he stopped talking to her entirely.

"Hey," Sophie whispered to her as they neared rehearsal, "what do you think about helping me and some other girls teach Brody Dixon a lesson?"

42

EVE

WINSTON: **k sorry to write you so early but I read all the stuff u sent and its amazing**

EVE: **oh my gosh no**

WINSTON: **it doesnt sound like the kind of poetry you read in class you know**

EVE: **thanks?**

WINSTON: **i mean it sounds like you're writing in a diary or something, but in a way thats better than that. all these words that put images in your head and stuff. send me more send me all of it**

EVE: **haha ur so nice**

WINSTON: **im glad you think so**

EVE: ☺

WINSTON: ☺

EVE: **ready for tonight?**

WINSTON: **I hope so**

43

SOPHIE

Break a leg, kiddo read the postcard from Seattle.

Did her dad know you didn't say that to the hair-and-makeup person? Or did you? Really, she didn't know. So much was new to her lately.

They'd already done their first show, and now it was time for closing night. The big event.

She'd be sad when it was over. To be honest, she really enjoyed her job. It was like everything she'd learned about dressing up as Sophie Kane could be used to dress up other characters. Why did Nessa have to be right about so much stuff?

Nessa had been helping Sophie with Spanish, and Sophie had been helping Nessa with math. And on opening night, she'd found herself applauding after Nessa's song like a proud mother or something.

These girls surprised her. Lara was so strategic and organized and put together, and Erin was so quick and funny. She seemed to always know the perfect comeback for anything. And Amina had convinced all the Roses and Brody's friends to come to the closing night instead of opening. Sophie asked how she did it, and Amina just answered, "Magic." There was a lot to learn about Amina, Sophie saw. About everyone.

As Sophie packed her stuff to go to the show, her mom and Bella got dressed. Her mom took the night off to come, which was silly. It was no big deal. And she told her mom as much, but her mom said, "Nope, nope, nope, I wouldn't miss it for the world," and made it happen. She'd come to the track meet, too. Sophie hoped that meant her dad had sent some extra money so the missed shifts didn't hurt them too much.

"I can't believe you know the *lead*!" Bella trilled as they all packed into the car.

"Yeah, we're good friends," she heard herself saying.

Each night, starting at dress rehearsal, she'd done Brody's and Nessa's makeup. The school didn't have a dressing room or anything, so the whole cast used the choir room. The leads did their hair and makeup off in the corner. The ensemble splayed their stuff all over the rest of the room, and waited there before the show and in between each group song.

In the makeup corner that night, Sophie saved Brody's and Nessa's makeup for last, so it would be fresh, and so they could warm up their voices until the very last minute.

Unfortunately, a terrible error in the song "The Wells Fargo Wagon" had been made the night before. The harmony sounded off or something, and Mr. Rhodes called everyone except Harold Hill to come to the stage for a quick rehearsal about a half hour before the curtain went up. That left Sophie alone in the room with Brody Dixon.

She fought the urge to paint his face like a clown or to give him overly eye-lined eyes. Her impulse to do an excellent job won out.

Sophie and Brody hadn't been alone since . . . well, since before the list came out, when they'd sat in his room together.

She remembered that right before he'd tried to kiss her, he'd told her something like, "It's wild, because you're, like, the prettiest girl I've ever met, but you're also so, so smart." And she'd thought it was this huge compliment, replaying it in her head over and over, thinking his smile meant he'd be her boyfriend by the end of eighth grade, and that they'd go into high school and run everything together.

But that hadn't been a compliment. It shouldn't have been "wild" for a girl to be pretty *and* smart, or *any* combination of *anything.*

And he'd never be her boyfriend.

As she silently dabbed his face with stage makeup, knowing that night was his night to be taken down, she wanted the truth.

"So did you ever actually like me?" Sophie asked, her neutral face revealing none of the bravery that the question took.

Brody briefly glanced up from the game on his phone.

"I mean . . ." She let the powder brush lower to her side. "Were you just trying to get the girl everybody else liked? Or something like that? Like with Eve?"

Brody half laughed, half grunted. "Aw, man, you've got me all figured out."

Sophie raised an eyebrow. "Just be straight with me!"

He went back to his game. "It's all no big deal, Soph. God."

She put her powder brush down in her makeup kit, snatched his phone, and held it behind her back. "No! You are going to explain yourself to me!" she demanded.

"Come on, give it back!" He started to stand to reach it, but she put up a hand gesturing for him to back off. He stayed seated.

"Why should I give it back? Because I'll find proof on

here that you're LordTesla?" she challenged him. "We were right all along, huh? You wanted to date Eve, a nerd, after you gave up on me, so you made the list? She pushed you off at the dance, so you turned on her, too? Just like you turned on me?"

Brody's low snicker turned into a full-on laugh, and his hands rested on his belly. "You are just too much, Sophie Kane."

"*Explain yourself.*" Sophie haphazardly pressed buttons on his phone like she could figure out the password to open it if she just tapped on it enough. "Or, I swear, I will—"

"What?" Brody leaned back in his chair in his brown salesman costume. "What will you do? Something about Nessa and her little picture of my coat?"

Sophie's hands froze.

"So what?" Brody went on. "That picture proves nothing."

Sophie felt herself begin to droop. He knew the plan. Of course he did. He always ended up on top.

"You just couldn't take a joke. That's why you're all"—he motioned to her slightly less than 'perfect' attire, the attire she *liked*, and her newly free hair—"like this?"

"No. No, actually, you're wrong." She remained steadfast.

"Am I?" he challenged her.

"Yes. And I like myself like this."

Brody slouched in his chair, suddenly looking much smaller. "*I didn't write the stupid list, okay?* I know you all think that I did. But I didn't." He shook his head. "You are so self-absorbed, did you know that?"

Brody smacked his forehead and his hand slid down, covering his mouth for a brief moment until he let it drop.

"What does it matter," he said to himself. "My dad's not coming, anyway."

"Your dad's not coming to the show? Why?"

Brody shook his head slightly and then slid farther into the chair, his legs sprawling out in front of him. "He thinks it's stupid. And it is. Give me back my *phone*," he groaned.

"Well, I'm sorry," Sophie said, unable to help herself. "My dad isn't coming, either."

Brody didn't seem to hear her. "My *phone*!"

"You don't have to be like your dad, you know," Sophie offered.

"Ha," he sneered. "Great advice. Thanks."

Sophie took a step closer to him.

"I'm sorry, okay?" He stood up. "But whatever. We are what people expect of us, right?"

"Brody—" She tried to stop him.

He snatched his phone back from her.

"Brody—" And again, she tried to make him face her, listen to her, but he turned to walk away.

"See ya."

As he stormed off, Nessa walked back in.

"Who died?" she asked.

The sixth and seventh grade ensembles came barging in after her, twirling and giggling and chatting.

Sophie launched herself toward the door, trying to get past them. "You didn't let me finish!" she yelled toward Brody, meaning that she hadn't completed his makeup, but also that she hadn't gotten all the answers she needed. But he was off.

"His dad's not coming to the show," Sophie whispered to Nessa. "That's pretty sad, right?"

"Oh." Nessa's jaw dropped. "Yeah, that's awful." Nessa glanced off toward where he'd stormed away. "At least his dad won't see him put into handcuffs and taken to middle school prison . . . That's what'll happen, right?"

Sophie allowed herself to smile, and she almost responded, "I don't think he wrote the list," but she couldn't do it.

She couldn't make herself save him.

44

EVE

Eve sat up in the lighting booth with Winston.

Below them, she saw a couple dozen masked girls in the audience. Her mask was pushed up on her hair.

"So tonight's the night," she said.

"Mm-hmm." Winston focused on dimming the lights as the audience applauded and a bunch of kids dressed in black came onstage to move set pieces around.

Nessa and Brody entered the stage for the scene that led into their big duet, "Till There Was You."

Eve leaned in to Winston to whisper, "My favorite part."

He smiled at her, and even in the dark of the booth, she

could see his skin turn crimson. "I think I've seen it about five times too many," he said with a chuckle.

Abe thought Winston was "a good guy," he'd said. And it was true. He'd never be the kind of boy to text her stuff that freaked her out, or laugh at her as she walked by, or tease her during laps in PE. And not just her—anybody! He would never hurt anybody.

She'd shown him her poetry. He'd liked it. And she believed him.

Did she like him, in that way? She didn't know for sure.

She wanted to think about it. That was all. Think about the possibility.

With Brody, it had all been really fast, and strange, and not . . . What was the right word? Warm. It hadn't been warm enough.

"Winston?"

She saw his hands freeze on the switchboard.

Nessa began to sing.

"I want to tell you something."

She saw him hold his breath.

"Thank you for helping us."

"No," he whispered back, a little louder than he should have.

"Shhh." She giggled.

He didn't laugh with her. "Don't give me any credit. I didn't get the IP address. I didn't do anything."

"Okay, but you cared about people getting hurt. Even when you weren't one of those people who was hurt. That's so . . . nice."

Winston shook his head, as if she'd said something utterly wrong. He went back to the lights to hit a cue.

The duet soared, Nessa's voice bouncing around every corner of the auditorium.

Soon, Nessa would reveal Brody's crimes to the school.

In the meantime, Nessa sang flawlessly, her whole face lighting up, her beauty shimmering outward toward the entire room.

"I'm not nice, okay?" he mumbled.

"Winston?" Eve leaned in closer to him. "What's wrong?"

"Nothing."

The song faded and the audience applauded. Only two more songs before curtain call. Before they knew it, students' phones would buzz like they had in October, and Brody would be the object of all the gawking and staring for once.

"Eve," Winston said. It felt like the first time he'd said her name, and she turned to him. His eyes remained forward, facing the conclusion barreling toward them.

"I know who wrote the list. And it wasn't Brody."

45

SOPHIE

From the wings, Sophie watched the show go on.

She thought of what Brody said. *We are what people expect of us, right?*

And she thought of the names on the library sign-in:

Caleb Rhines 7:15 A.M.
Winston Byrd 7:20 A.M.

She thought of the mornings she'd come in by 7:10 A.M. for swim practice in seventh grade. Some kids whose parents worked early were dropped off for breakfast an hour before the homeroom bell rang. The only places they were allowed to go to were sports practices, the cafeteria to eat, or the library.

She tried to remember who she'd seen back then. Rose Reed, definitely. Curtis Milford. Miranda Garland. Caleb Rhines. Winston Byrd.

Brody hadn't written the list. He hadn't pretended to be Caleb or Winston, thinking through how to cover his every move like a supervillain. Plus, the librarian would have known him. Everyone knew Brody Dixon. Writing in another name wouldn't have worked.

It was Caleb or Winston. Or Caleb *and* Winston. But why?

As Nessa and Brody sang "Till There Was You," their harmonies floating through the air and brightening the stage like fireflies, Sophie wondered if she should stop Nessa.

Brody hadn't written the list, it was true, but he was most likely guilty of spray painting the locker. And he had done even worse stuff!

Was there suspension enough for breaking people down like he did?

No.

Curtain call was close. Maybe she had to make this decision

with Nessa. As the song ended, she tried to signal to Nessa that they had to talk, but there was no time.

There was no time to turn back.

Revenge would happen, but maybe not justice. Or were they the same thing? Sophie didn't know anymore.

46

• • • • • • • • • • • •

EVE

"It was Caleb," Winston told her. "I watched him do it."

He held her hand and begged her not to leave.

The voices onstage melded with Winston's pleading whisper, and it all felt like a dream.

"You know how Caleb was my best friend."

She nodded.

"I know you understand. You also have a best friend like him, someone you've known forever. But I don't have a brother or sister. Caleb was that for me."

"Winston . . . ," she started to say, to stop him. She had to leave. She had to talk to Nessa.

"Okay. Wait." He took a breath. "Everything I told you about myself was true. School was brutal for me. Caleb knew I was a target for guys like Brody, so going into middle school he became friends with him. He said it was to protect us both. But I found out that to be protected from guys like that, you have to *become* guys like that. And I couldn't. But for Caleb . . . it seemed easy. He liked feeling, I dunno, in charge. And until this year, it wasn't so bad. He worked on our robot project with me after school; he didn't talk about girls all day long or something. But eighth grade? First, he got obsessed with Amina, saying all day how gorgeous she was and stuff, then he said Brody had told him she was 'crazy,' and so he started to get all obsessed with Rose. And he just . . . disappeared." Winston spoke in a rush, the words pouring out of him as though, if he stopped speaking, she might leave.

"They'd text each other *all* day," he went on, hardly catching a breath. "He would laugh at me when I talked about stuff we both used to like. It was just Rose and Caleb, nonstop. But, like, I started to get it. I got why they liked each other. Because Rose was a girl version of Caleb. She wanted to be friends with Sophie Kane, and Caleb wanted to be friends with Brody Dixon, and that was all that mattered."

Eve nodded.

"So one day, Caleb told me to meet him at the library during breakfast. When I met him there, he was writing the"—Winston paused, like it was a bad word—"list. He told me he'd made the list for Rose and he was going to put her in the top five. He said she'd be so excited."

No, no. This couldn't be happening. Eve got up to leave.

"No, wait! I told him that it was a really bad idea. I swear. I told him that everyone would think she wrote it, and he was like, 'That's why I'm making her number four.'"

"*That's* why it was a bad idea?" Eve fought the urge to shriek.

Winston kept going. "He said that nobody would suspect number four wrote it. He put Sophie Kane as number two, and you as number one."

"But *why*?" she rasped.

"He said you . . . he said you had 'a body.'" Winston couldn't look at her, staring instead at the light switchboard. His words slowed. "He said over the summer you'd . . . changed."

Eve felt tears begin to shoot down her cheeks even as her face remained still and no sound came out.

"Eve, I'm so sorry. I didn't know you then."

"And why does it matter if you knew me or not?" Eve spoke in such a low whisper she couldn't be sure if Winston even heard her.

"I thought, 'Oh, that girl seems nice. Sure.' I thought you'd like it. I mean, I thought that any girl getting called the prettiest would be, like, the greatest thing ever for them. I actually even remember thinking that the only good part about what Caleb was doing was that"—he sighed—"that someone who wasn't popular would get such a big compliment. Like maybe it would change your life."

"It did," she whispered.

"I know, and I'm so sorry."

"Stop saying sorry."

"Okay. Okay." He rubbed his temples. Down below, Nessa sang.

"What happened next?" Eve asked. She had to know.

"I don't understand why he put certain girls in certain spots, exactly. He didn't want Lara on there because she 'seemed too full of herself' or something, and not Miranda Garland because she was annoying, and it went on and on, and I was hardly listening to him, I promise! I was just sitting there!"

Back to the switchboard. Adjust the lights. Then back to her.

"Listen, I knew from the day of the assembly that I was wrong about it being a great compliment. I knew it when I saw you run out. And I found your poem."

"What?" Eve said too loudly, and Winston put a finger to his mouth to quiet her. His shushing infuriated her. The tears stopped. She should leave. She needed to go. But he had more to say.

"It's in my backpack. Always," he said.

Eve vaguely remembered dropping some of her notebook pages on the way to the choir room that day. He'd read them?

"The poem . . . I mean, you were clearly really sad. I chased after you. Did you hear me calling you? Before you ran into the choir room? I spent weeks trying to figure out how to tell you who wrote it and say sorry. How to make it all go away."

Winston picked up his backpack and pulled out the poem, handing it to her. She saw her own handwriting. The first line began: *I am large. I contain . . .*

"I knew that I'd hurt you by not stopping him. So much. And I hurt so many people. And I really did want to take down Brody. Because he *is* a bad guy! I didn't lie—he *did* brag that he wrote the list! Who *would do* that? And he *ruined* Caleb! Look, I know I lied. I wanted to tell the truth . . . And then your friends got this idea that I know something about IP addresses? I'm into mechanical engineering, not computer science, so . . . I guess theater kids think all science is the same? I just went along with it, I don't know, I wanted to be there to help you, all of you, in some way . . ."

She could see that he knew he was losing her.

"And every time I wanted to tell you, every time I even brought it up to Caleb, Caleb told me I'd get expelled. And he saw that I was getting to know you. He told me my mom would never forgive me, and that you wouldn't, either!"

She could feel him trying to catch her eye, but she refused to look at him. The curtains wheeled in from the wings, marking the end of the show.

"And you're . . . wonderful. You're smart and talented and such a good friend and you think all these thoughts that no one else could think and . . . and I just—"

"Caleb was right," Eve interrupted him. "I won't ever forgive you."

She ran out of the booth. She had to get to Nessa.

47

NESSA

Nessa stood there, onstage for the curtain call, with her phone in her palm.

She saw Brody look out into the audience, searching the faces.

Was he looking for his dad? His fancy dad, who everyone knew was this big-time guy with lots of money and an actual model for a girlfriend (it was true—they'd seen her in a Kohl's catalog once), but who couldn't make the time to come see his kid be really good as the lead in a show? Even worse, what if he did have the time and didn't think it was a big deal?

Out in the crowd she saw her mom and dad. Her mom was

blowing her nose and wiping away tears with the same tissue (ew), and her dad was applauding as if he'd just heard music for the first time. And Nessa couldn't help it, she beamed at them and waved. So unprofessional, but she had to.

She waved with the phone in her hand.

Brody looked at her hand, and then at her face. And something in his eyes stopped her thumb from hitting send. When he sang with her, even though his voice was brittle, those eyes filled up with feeling. When he saw the phone, and looked out at the audience without his dad in it, it was like his eyes went blank.

She glanced at Lara, who had an excited grin on her face, and at Erin, who couldn't have looked more ready to put their plan into action, and at Sophie, who was mouthing something at her from the wings, waving her hands in the air, and at Principal Yu, who was heading toward the stage with flowers for Mr. Rhodes.

And as she was about to put the phone in her pocket to spare Brody, she heard him speak.

"Hey! Hey!" he hollered, quieting the audience down except for some people wondering aloud what was going on. "Hey, everyone. I have an announcement to make. It was me. I wrote the list. And I lied and said Eve did it. And I spray painted her locker, too. I'm really sorry."

Audible shock filled the auditorium. And then boos. And someone screamed, "I HATE YOU, BRODY DIXON!"

And chaos began.

The entire ensemble dissolved into chatter, Principal Yu ran to the front of the stage to try to take control, and Brody stood there, staring out at everyone, at no one who really mattered, Nessa guessed. The person who mattered would get a call in a few minutes, she was sure about that.

Nessa caught Sophie's eye finally, and Sophie mouthed something.

Nessa mouthed back, "What do I do? Do I bow again?" She acted out another little curtsy.

Sophie gestured for her to get off the stage. Lara and Erin, too.

"Coming through!" Erin yelled, and they all made their way into the wings.

Kids ran by them and pulled out their phones to enthusiastically text. A few took videos of Brody walking offstage with Principal Yu and Mr. Rhodes.

Sophie held on to Nessa by the arm, and all of the Shieldmaiden girls leaned in.

"He didn't write the list," Sophie told them. "I'm sure of it."

They watched him walk away. He seemed undisturbed. At peace.

"Why'd he say it, then?" Lara asked.

"It's what people expected of him, anyway," Sophie said with a sigh, as if surrendering.

"I thought this would feel good." Nessa put her head on Sophie's shoulder. "But I'm just tired."

48

• • • • • • • • • • • •

EVE

The world had flipped upside down. She couldn't think straight. She couldn't piece together who was guilty of what and why.

Eve heard an eruption inside the auditorium before she made it inside to warn Nessa.

Soon after, the doors of the theater burst open and she saw Principal Yu and Mr. Rhodes leading Brody toward the second floor, presumably to Principal Yu's office.

"Wait!" Eve hollered. "Wait, Principal Yu!"

They continued to hurry off and within seconds were out of sight.

Moments after, the crowd trickled out of the side doors, and the cast came to meet them, all babbling and bustling, full of "Can you believe its?" and "I knew its!" and "Best show EVERs!"

As Nessa stepped into view, large swaths of the crowd cheered.

"Oh, stop, stop." Nessa glowed.

Eve spotted Sophie's little sister, Bella, asking for an autograph.

Sophie waved to Eve, motioning her over. When they reached each other, Eve grasped onto Sophie like she was a piece of land in the middle of the ocean.

"Winston and Caleb did it," she whispered in Sophie's ear.

Sophie pulled away, still holding Eve's elbows, and her face held no surprise.

"You knew about Winston." Eve stared in wonder.

"Let's just say I had an idea."

"I don't know what to do," Eve confessed.

"I think he was honestly on our side." Sophie patted her arm. "He just messed up really, really bad."

"But what about Brody?"

"I know," Sophie whispered. "We have to tell, right?"

"Sophie, honey, it all looked great!" Sophie's mom came to hug her, and Eve slipped out of sight.

Eve made her way to the front of the school. Before she could reach the entrance, an enormous swarm of girls surrounded her, all wearing masks.

"I believed you the whole time!" one of them said.

"We shouldn't have to worry about how we look all the time!" a younger voice cried out to her.

"Look!" A girl held up a plastic bag filled with superhero masks. "I've been giving them to everybody!"

Eve looked around and saw them. Girls with masks in every color dotted the crowd.

"I'm tired of them looking at us."

"Of them *judging* us!"

"And thinking we can be *ranked*! Like it's a game!"

"Yeah! We are taking ourselves out of the running!"

The voices continued, and behind a couple of the kids Eve saw Miranda Garland come up to the girl passing out masks and grab one for herself. Miranda saw Eve watching her and waved the mask as if to say hello.

"You were right this whole time!" the girls kept repeating.

And Eve tried to say, "No, maybe not," but they weren't listening. She told them thanks and bye, and she rushed out of the school into the freezing air. She sat where she'd once sat with Brody, except now the bench felt ice cold. She pulled her down coat tight around herself.

Eve's phone buzzed and she glanced at it. It was a text from Miranda Garland: **hey just wanted to say im super sorry**

Then Curtis:

sry i was mean to you

Unknown number:

hey sorry i didnt mean the stuff i said

Unknown number:

sorry for wht happnd to u

And then Nessa:

Hey. Sorry for not getting the mask thing. Or the Brody thing. We ok?

One night and so many sorrys.

Eve wished for snow. Snow would lighten the night sky. Snow would illuminate the concrete. She wanted something beautiful, right then and there.

Abe swerved up to the school a few minutes later.

"Hop in, Dickinson," he said.

Eve readied herself for bed.

So who was she meant to be, a nobody or a somebody? Were there only two choices?

Eve's mother was surely down the hall praying for the sick.

For her brother's safety as he drove. For who knows what else. And then she'd whisper the *Sh'ma*. A poem itself. Like all prayers were.

The scenes of autumn replayed themselves in Eve's head. And the words of poets who'd lived hundreds of years ago, with problems much bigger than her own, repeated themselves again and again in her mind like a soundtrack for her life.

How dreary to be somebody. How public, like a frog. To tell one's name, the livelong June, to an admiring bog . . .

I am the daughter of Earth and Water, And the nursling of the Sky . . .

I am large, I contain multitudes . . .

She still didn't know what she contained. She just knew the million things that other people assumed she was. Her parents. Brody. Sophie. Winston. Even Nessa. All she knew was that she wasn't who any of them thought she should be. She was something else entirely. But what?

She *contained multitudes*. That was it. She contained a poet, the prettiest girl, a plain Jane, a girl who looked for the beauty in little things, who liked her quiet room, who could disappear within herself, maybe for too long sometimes, who wanted some attention, but not too much, a person who loved her one best friend but had started to like having more of them. She wasn't one thing. None of them were.

They were more than numbers on a list, more than their cafeteria tables, or their hobbies, or their groups.

Within each of them were a million universes.

Multitudes.

And with that thought, Eve dropped her mask into the waste basket. She picked up her phone, ignoring the dozens of notifications from the Shieldmaidens group chat. She wrote, **I'm okay. Busy. What an intense night. You were all amazing.**

Eve wrote privately to Nessa: **Of course we're ok. There's a lot I didn't get, too.**

She grabbed last year's yearbook, sat at her desk, and opened a notebook. She went through every name, endowing each with a sliver of insight, painting a piece of every one with words, able only to merely graze over the tiniest star of the universes within each, but opening the door for more.

Then Eve typed it up, took a screenshot, posted it online, softly recited the *Sh'ma*, and went to sleep.

49

SOPHIE

They all woke up to the poem. Or was it a poem? Sophie didn't really know.

It was a *list*, made up of one or two lines about each girl in the eighth grade.

> *Lara Alexander is elegance in motion. I imagine her in lengthy gowns, holding court in palace gardens, keeping cruelty forever locked out of the castle gates.*

> *Amina Alvi shimmers. We watch her closely, and it's hard not to, because when she blinks it's like her*

eyelids open and close their doors on the moonlight. Maybe that light is her kindness.

Nessa Flores-Brady, a walking, beating heart, who sings like all hearts sing, with wonder, with melancholy. I always thought I knew the story behind each scab and scar, but now, today, I know there's more.

Miranda Garland, she knows all this better than I because she watches the world and notes its details. A mind like hers could paint people, hallways, planets from memory.

Liv Henry, I see her surrounded by floating numbers and bubbling potions, rewiring a galaxy. She holds supernovas within, black holes and newborn stars.

Erin O'Brien has discovered the answer to questions we haven't even thought of yet. Sometimes, when she thinks no one's looking, I see the tips of her mouth rise up in a smile. What's her daydream?

A tiger lily is orange and so is Rose Reed, bright in the bland gray of middle school, a flame in the ice. She will take over the world if she wants, molding earth with bare hands.

Hayley Salem, floating on clouds, grounded by legs strong as a gazelle's, she can run and fly. I see her giggle and want to know if she ever frowns, and why.

And who am I?

I am large. I am a million somebodys. I'm Eve Hoffman. The daughter of Deb and Joe. Not Number One or Liar or Body. I am a girl of contradictions. I drink English class like it's lemonade in August, but my words stumble when I speak. I am constantly baffled and afraid, and sometimes, just sometimes, I am incredibly strong.

I contain multitudes, we all contain multitudes, we are a million things unfolding eternally and we'll never even know our own full stories.

You are not a number. You are not a body.

What's one piece of one more universe inside you? What are your multitudes?

And below, the comments section had dozens of comments. And then, within a few hours, a hundred. And then a hundred more, from seventh and eighth graders and girls who didn't even go to their school. But . . . they weren't quite comments. More like confessions—the things people hid, or that didn't fit with their group or face. They weren't quite poetry, like Eve's post. But maybe they were?

I'm afraid of spirits. Like . . . I seriously can't breathe when I think of haunted houses. But, also, sometimes I wonder if it's because I can secretly, like, talk to them or something. Like I'm a ghost hunter.

My mom is my hero. I wrote a paper saying it was Susan B. Anthony, but it's my mom.

I love my hair. It's frizzy and all this "bad" stuff or whatever and I know I'm supposed to hate it, but I just love it. I think it's cute. And I'm not going to change it.

My dad took me to a psychic and she told me my soul is the color of lime. I don't believe in psychics, but I believe that.

My brother gets really sick sometimes. He has this disease called sickle cell. We spend a lot of time in the hospital, but we try to make it fun for him. He's only eleven, but he's tougher than anybody. Sometimes I'm sad about that at school, and people just think I'm stuck-up. I'm not. I'm just worried.

I write My Little Pony fan fiction. But it's not stupid. It's about what they really feel, as if they were real people. And no one should laugh at me about that! It makes me happy!

And on and on and on. People kept adding more, secrets and stories and facts into the hundreds. Some wrote from anonymous accounts, but many didn't. Each time Sophie checked, there were more. And on each comment were a dozen responses. Girls saying "I feel that way, too!" or "I'm so sorry about your brother" or "I want a lime soul! So neat!"

The list had officially been replaced. And this time, every girl was on it.

Sophie read and reread her favorite line in what Eve had written about her:

Sophie Kane, a girl with the courage of an army inside her.

That night, as she sat with her mom by the sewing machine, working on their new project—a red jacket for Bella for the spring—Sophie Kane announced, "Mom. I'd like to have friends from Ford over during winter break. They won't think less of me."

Her mom stopped fiddling with the spool and sighed. "Honey, I—" she began, like Sophie didn't already know.

"Mama," she said, calling her what she'd called her until she was just a little older than Bella. "I know you didn't want my friends coming over here because you just didn't want me to be bullied."

Her mom opened her mouth as if to speak, but didn't.

"But these kids . . . they're not like that. And I'm not ashamed of Silver Ledge or anything. I'm proud of you."

Her mom didn't have to say "I love you" or "I'm proud of you, too," because her eyes did. Because everything she did in life showed Sophie how she felt about her.

"Okay, baby girl. Okay." After a beat, her mom lifted up a bag of bright red buttons. "Perfect for Bel, right?"

"Perfect." Sophie smiled.

50

NESSA

On New Year's Eve, it snowed. Flakes dotted Eve's curls as Eve and Nessa hopped out of Nessa's dad's car.

"Are you ready to see him if he comes?" Nessa asked her.

"I think so." Eve gazed up at the sky. "I love how purply orange the sky gets when the snow falls at night."

"It's nice." Back to business. "Are you gonna forgive him, because he knew not what he did?"

Eve laughed.

Another car pulled up, and Lara and Erin tapped on the windows from inside Erin's parents' car.

Erin came down the ramp with a noisemaker in her mouth and a party hat.

"She's been blowing that thing nonstop. Please help me," Lara deadpanned. Lara wore a white flower headpiece in her hair.

"You're the classiest person I know," Nessa told her, nodding to the flower.

"And you're the cutest," Lara said, taking Nessa's hand and twirling her around.

"Is you-know-who coming?" Lara asked as they all headed into the building together.

"I think so," Nessa answered.

"His apology was really nice," Erin told them. "I milked it for all it was worth. He felt really bad."

"Yeah, he wrote me an actual letter," Lara said. "In the *mail*. I liked the whole pigeon-carrier feel to it."

Nessa laughed.

They spotted the right entrance.

"Guys!" they heard a voice call out from a few yards away.

Amina bounded toward them. "Wow! The snow!" she said, clearly still a bit nervous around them. Weather talk always meant someone was nervous.

"Want a noisemaker?" Erin held one out.

"Ooh, yes, please." Amina took it.

"Don't forget me!" Nessa put out her palm.

And as Sophie came on the intercom to say, "Guys? Is it you?" they all blew into the speaker, so loudly that probably the whole neighborhood could hear them.

51

SOPHIE

Her mom had cleaned the place like a fiend, and Sophie understood. But when her mom started dusting the lampshades, it was Sophie's duty to stop her.

"Mom. Enough. Go take a nap or something!"

When the girls arrived, Sophie twirled as they entered. "My newest creation!"

She'd made a black dress out of a nightgown from the thrift store, an Audrey Hepburn thing, but with a frill on the bottom and trimmings of lace around the sleeves. She looked fantastic. Her muscles showed in it, but she was trying not to mind. It was hard. But she was trying.

"Awesome!" Nessa high-fived her.

"You are seriously talented," Lara declared, and looked at her from all sides. "Well done!"

"Hannah begged to come see Bella, but she's not allowed to stay up until midnight," Eve told her. "You look so cool," she added.

Sophie motioned Eve toward her and Bella's bedroom and pointed inside. Bella lay spread out in her clothes on her bed, fast asleep.

"They'll have to hang out sometime," Sophie whispered. "You look awesome, by the way." Sophie's hand shot to cover her mouth, and she added, "Not that it matters what you wear!" She had a new rule for herself to make people's looks one of the last things she ever pointed out. But Eve did look awesome. She wore her old black jeans like she used to, but her top, a lavender sweater, fit her just right.

"You look like"—Sophie thought for a moment to find the right word—"you."

"Popcorn time!" Sophie's mom yelled from the kitchen.

After an hour or so of sitting on the couch, half watching the lead-up to the ball drop, and chatting nonstop about the past three months, Sophie heard the buzzer.

She jumped up. "Got it!"

She opened the door a crack and watched him walk

down the hallway toward her, his nose nearly purple from the cold.

"Hey. Don't worry, you're welcome here," she made sure to tell him before he came in. "Join us!" She heard herself sound chirpier than ever. So embarrassing. But she was happy, she supposed. Maybe being happy made people chirpy.

"More friends?" she heard her mom say. "Where have you been hiding these people?"

Sophie shrugged and looked around at her very full apartment.

52

EVE

Winston stood in the doorway. She had known he would come, but it still felt strange to see him. She hadn't seen him since he'd told her what he'd done, and she didn't know if he would look different to her after that.

As Winston remained frozen by the door, Nessa yelled out, "Just get in here!"

Eve got up to talk to him as he took off his gloves and untied his scarf. He remained out of earshot from the rest of the group. With the doorway on one end of the room and the couch and TV on the other, everyone could see what was going on, but not hear it.

"Hey." Eve nodded to Winston.

"Hey."

Eve could feel Nessa glancing over at them and waiting to see what happened.

"So . . ." She felt relieved to find she wasn't blushing.

"I loved what you wrote," he said.

"Thanks."

"I love your . . ." He paused and pressed his lips together like he did when he thought hard about something, focused on the mission, or the locker, or the lights. "Your voice."

"Thank you," Eve repeated. "It felt good to use it."

"I bet," he uttered under his breath. "Look . . . I've apologized to each person in there except you. And that's because I betrayed you worst of all. I made you think I was safe, and I was the opposite of that."

"What did your mom do when you told her?" From the little bit she'd seen of Winston's mom at the assembly, she could only imagine how intimidating she must have been after he admitted what he did.

"Let's just say I'm only allowed to come here tonight because I'm apologizing, and I won't be out in the world much this winter. Or this *year*. She seemed . . . I think the right word would probably be 'heartbroken.'" He took a breath. "When I told her, she said, 'You know what you need to do,' and she wrote down Principal Yu's number for me. And then she left the room." Winston bit his lip. "Anyway, Principal Yu was pretty nice about it. Disappointed, though. She said she had to do some thinking about how to handle it, so . . . my fate is uncertain. Caleb's, too." After a beat, he added, "She told me how you guys had already told her about Brody. How it wasn't him."

At that, Eve smiled. They'd gone to Principal Yu the day after the show to tell her they knew Brody didn't do it. They didn't say how they knew. For some reason, though, Principal Yu hadn't probed them further. She'd said she understood and thanked them.

"What'll happen to Brody, you think?" Eve wondered aloud.

"He'll get in trouble for the stuff he did do, I bet. I also heard he might transfer to Greenmount."

Eve allowed a few moments of silence to pass between them.

"I stood by and watched Caleb write it," Winton said finally. "I could have stopped him."

"Yes," Eve said.

"I'm so sorry." Winston met her eyes. "I'm so sorry, Eve."

"I know you are."

Though their friends' roars of laughter were only yards

away, at that moment it felt like miles. Like she and Winston were on their own island.

"Guys! The ball is gonna drop soon! Come on!" one of the girls called out to them.

Winston hadn't even taken his boots off, she noticed, as if he'd assumed he'd be kicked out.

Eve turned to join the group.

"You coming?" she asked him.

After a brief pause, he slipped off his boots and followed.

Erin sat right next to the couch, and the rest of them all squeezed in so tight on it that Sophie ended up on Nessa's lap and Eve's legs rested over Amina's. Lara stood up and said, "I can't do this," and sat cross-legged on the floor.

"Well, hi, Byrd!" Nessa reached over to pat his back as a greeting.

"Hi, everybody," Winston said in a shy mumble.

"Everybody do their resolutions?" Eve grabbed the paper and colored pens from the coffee table and handed some to Winston.

"Yup. I'm going to get the lead in *Oklahoma!* this spring," Nessa announced.

They all burst out laughing.

"I don't think that's a resolution, hon," Sophie said. "That's, like, a goal."

"A resolution is a goal for how you're going to *change*," Lara told her. "Like, for me, I'm going to care less about what people think."

"*Such a good one*!" Sophie grabbed her own paper. "Give me a pen. I have to add that."

Eve wrote down that she would write once a day. She'd share her writing with someone. And she'd show her true self to the world. Whatever that meant in the year to come.

Eve looked over at Winston and saw him writing furiously, filling up the page.

After a few minutes of watching ball-drop banter on TV, Sophie spoke. "You all hear there's another list?"

Nessa nodded, her expression grim. "And Rose Reed is number one. Blech. Not 'blech' to Rose Reed. 'Blech' to more lists."

"Plus, being number one's not so easy," Eve added.

"True." Sophie caught her eye.

"It's really sad," Amina jumped in. "I think. Am I right? It's sad?" She looked from person to person, maybe wondering if she'd said the wrong thing.

"'Sad' is the only word for it, in my opinion!" Lara pronounced before digging into some guacamole.

"Hey, maybe we should try to talk to her," Nessa suggested.

"Always worth a try," Sophie said with a look of determination.

Erin threw a popcorn kernel toward the ceiling, then opened her mouth wide and caught it.

"No way! Skills!" Nessa tried to do the same thing, and it landed in her eye.

"All right, guys, it's almost midnight—which channel do we want to go with?" Sophie fiddled with the remote.

Eve had read some wonderful New Year's poems online earlier that day. She began to recite one: "There's a poem by Ella Wheeler Wilcox that goes: *What can be said in New Year rhymes, that's not been said a thousand times?*"

"Here we go . . . ," Nessa groaned.

"What? I'm a poet!"

Nessa sighed. "Fine. Go on."

"*The new years come, the old years go. We know we dream, we dream we know. We rise up laughing with the light. We lie down weeping with the night. We hug the world until it stings . . .*"

"Okay, please get to the ending, Evie, please," Nessa pleaded.

"Okay, okay!" Eve skipped ahead. "*We laugh, we weep, we hope, we fear, and that's the burden of the year.*"

"Nice!" Amina encouraged her.

Eve had lost the rest of them to the TV. "Thanks, Amina."

Winston leaned in to Eve and said softly, "That poem? It's really pretty."

"Isn't it?" She smiled at him.

"Okay, everybody!" Nessa stood up, and they all held hands. "It's time!"

And, together, they counted down to a new beginning:

Ten, nine, eight, seven, six, five, four, three, two, one . . .

ACKNOWLEDGMENTS

Eternal thanks to Melissa Edwards, my outstanding agent, for wholeheartedly supporting this book from the moment I had the idea for it. Thank you to Connie Hsu and Megan Abbate for so sensitively and masterfully helping me find the heart and soul of this story. Thank you to Madison Furr, Mekisha Telfer, Patricia McHugh, Nancee Adams-Taylor, Jessica Warren, and Taylor Pitts for your expertise and hard work, and to the entire team at Roaring Brook Press for your support. And thank you to Cassie Gonzales and Anjali Mehta for the cover of my dreams!

Nick Shoda, your insights made this book better in every way before I'd even written a word. Thank you.

Laura Hoffman-Hernandez, you and your beautiful

family have my endless gratitude for sharing your stories with me.

Paul Gross, thank you for helping me deepen Eve's world.

Thank you to Natalie and Audrey Compare for being two of my most valued readers. You are both destined for greatness, but, more importantly, you are infinitely kind. I can't wait to see what you choose to do in this world as you grow up.

Thank you to Risa Sang-urai Harms, Sasha Lazare, Brita Loftus, and Kristina Tomlinson for sharing your memories of middle school and girlhood with me.

Alexander Whatley, thank you for debating gender politics (as well as everything else) with me for going on twenty years. I've learned a lot.

Kelly Granito, thank you for helping me find the right perspective for this story.

Thank you to Laura Mulcahy for standing by me in middle school and forever after.

Thank you to Margery Ross for making my husband read *Are You There God? It's Me, Margaret* when he was a kid. You raised a mensch. Thank you to David Ross for trading outraged emails with me.

Thank you to my dad, Ernest P. Young, for your gentle nature, your inspirational activist past and present, and for reading my work with such love. Thank you to my mom,

M. Brady Mikusko, for infusing my life with anger at injustice and for letting me know that my voice has value.

Thank you to my niece, Claudia Maschio, for keeping me in touch with the reality of life as a young, strong girl.

Thank you to Aunt Kate, Aunt Suzi, Sarah, and my late grandma, Alice, for the lifelong coven.

Thank you to my love, Jonathan, for keeping me in the light.

And thank you to my precious daughters, Ingrid and Simone. I hope the world grows along with you. We will never stop trying to make it better.

AUTHOR'S NOTE

It happened to me. In my life, the lists took a slightly different form, and the texts existed as written notes, but they created the same feelings of pressure, confusion, and shame. Some of these characters' experiences mirror mine quite literally: the water thrown on Eve's chest, Principal Yu's encounters with Wes, and the endless accusations of a stuffed bra, for example. In all honesty, some moments of harassment and sexism felt too painful to even include. Throughout the years, my strategies of handling such treatment shifted. At times, I felt like Eve—desperate to hide, to disappear into myself, to escape the outside gaze. In other moments, I lived as Sophie—playing the game, and working hard to reflect what I'd been told would help me conquer the system. I figured it was better to fit into what I felt I *should* be rather than discover my own truth. And, at times, I was Nessa. I ignored the prevailing power structure and understood my worth, even as I felt sorrow and rage that others couldn't see it.

In some notable ways, I was Winston, too. I had moments in which I could have stood up for others, but the fear of being bullied myself took precedence. And, of course, like all the characters, I wasn't immune to judging girls on their appearances, or letting that be the first thing I saw. In fact, to this day, I still have moments in which I struggle with all of this. In a world that too often presents "good looks" as girls' and women's central quality, and defines "good looks" in a *very* particular and narrow way, I continue to work on tuning out the noise. I try to remember the oft-shared wisdom that in a world that feeds on self-doubt, loving oneself is a revolutionary act. But it's not easy.

I didn't know it in middle school, but I know now that I'm not alone. In the end of this story, I wanted to give my characters a taste of that knowledge. They conclude their journey as a community of friends who value one another and stand proudly together against the pressures of the world.

They are not alone. I am not alone. You are not alone. We'll find our way through it together.

Learn about your rights and how to take action against sexual harassment in schools here:

equalrights.org/legal-help/know-your-rights/sexual-harassment-at-school

nwlc.org/issue/sexual-harassment-assault-in-schools